Brody: Encouraged to Seek

The Barnabas Chronicles
Book 10

By

Ronna M. Bacon

1 Chronicles 16:11

Seek the Lord and His strength;

Seek His face continually.

Psalm 9:9-10

The LORD also will be a refuge for the oppressed, a refuge in times of trouble. And they that know your name will put their trust in you: for you, LORD, have not forsaken them that seek you.

NKJV

Table of Contents

Chapter 1

Tucking his pen back into his portfolio, Brody Corcoran glanced around the tastefully-furnished reception area of the business office that he found himself in. He was to meet with a Ker Deeks. *I wonder what he is like,* he wondered, trying not to listen to the voice of the lady who had answered the phone. He could not see her, but her low voice was melodious and drew him to want to meet her. He sighed. No, he decided, he would not have an adventure as nine of his friends from the Barnabas Foundation building had had. They had almost lost some of his friends and their ladies to death. It had been too close.

Shifting in his chair, Brody glanced at his watch. He had been early for his appointment, something that he was trying to change, but couldn't. He stood for a moment, moving to stare out of the window, watching the parking lot of the building. Located at the edge of a town near where he lived, Brody studied the area, a prickling sensation tingling at his neck. He didn't like that feeling. Not one bit, he decided.

He turned as he heard his name called and studied the young lady, around his age, he thought, as she approached him. Red gold hair. Dark gray eyes. Freckles sprinkled across her nose. He mentally shook his head. There was no way that she was real. This was the image of the lady that he had always thought he would find.

"Mr. Corcoran? I'm sorry. I was on a call that I just couldn't end. Please? This way?" She pointed to a conference room. "Have a seat. Can I offer you a coffee or tea?"

"No, thank you. I'm okay, but don't let me stop you from having something." He grinned at her, laughter for a moment sparkling in his deep blue eyes.

Ker Deeks studied the man in front of her. Tall, she thought, too tall. Dark brown hair. Blue eyes. *Dad, what did you do? You asked me to meet with him, and then you ducked out. I hope my suspicions are not correct, that you are trying to set me up.*

"No, that's okay. I'm Ker Deeks." She looked up at the silence and then smiled. "Expecting a male person? That would have been my father that you spoke with. He's out of the office, but you can speak to me. Or we can reschedule for when Dad is around."

Brody shook his head, desperate to collect his thoughts. "No, it's fine. I just wasn't expecting a lady."

Ker gave an unladylike snort, which caused Brody to grin in return. "Blame my brother. He wanted a younger brother and got me. He had already picked out the name. Mom and Dad just feminized it."

"Feminized it? Is there such a word?" Brody shook his head, dropping his face to hide his grin. *This was going to be an interesting meeting, wasn't it, Lord? And I can see Your hand in it already.* "Now, your father asked me to stop by. He said he had some documents that he needed to have drawn up?"

—

"He does." Ker reached for the folder she had placed on the table. "These are the ones that he is thinking of. Just for an explanation, Dad's business is highly confidential. He does searches for missing children and teens. He tries hard to keep out of the news. So far, we have managed to do that."

"I see. I wasn't aware of that. And you are in the office, then?"

Ker nodded. "Most of the time. Sometimes, if there is an emergency, and we can't get our teams to go in and bring out the children or teens from another area, I go in. We work closely with all law enforcement authorities and courts. We never go in without clearing it first. That's how Dad has always worked."

"Then, what forms are you needing to draw up? I am sure that you have had them already in place."

"We have." Ker sighed. "But for some reason, the law office that we usually work with has become difficult to do just that. There have been some changes in personnel. A new lawyer has been taken into the partnership there. Neither Dad, Keefe, or I trust him. There has been something off about him, and we just don't know what. I'm sorry. I shouldn't have said anything." She looked troubled.

"No, it's okay. It goes no further than our conversation here in this room. It just helps me to understand why you are looking for someone new. May I?" Brody reached for the papers, glancing through them, a frown on his face. "Have you used these yet?"

"No, not yet. Dad looked at them, and then he refused to. That's when he talked to Bruce Carey, asking if he knew someone who could look them over and then help us."

"Bruce? Your father knows him?"

"He does. They have been friends for years." Ker studied him, suddenly not sure of him. "You seem surprised."

"I shouldn't be. Bruce's son, Barnabas, asked me to come. I work for the Foundation, even though my employer is a firm of paralegals."

"You do? Then, that's why." Ker paused, her head turning as she heard a soft click of a door. "Excuse me for a moment? That's the back door. No one should be coming in there. Dad is away. Keefe is on vacation this week."

Brody was on his feet, a hand stopping her from moving forward. "Wait. Let me go, please?"

"It's not your office." Ker tried to disguise her discomfort at his stepping in.

"Doesn't matter. I won't let a lady go out into danger." Brody strode out of the room, heading for the back door, searching the offices as he passed them, not seeing anyone. He stood for a moment just inside the door of a large, multifunctional room, seeking to find the person or persons who had entered. He had no doubt that they were no longer alone in the office.

A scuffling sound behind him had him turning. Only he never made it all the way around. A blow to his head dropped him to his knees, his hands going out to stop himself from landing face down on the tiled floor. He vaguely heard Ker scream and then the sounds of a struggle. He was hauled to his feet, swaying as his vision darkened before he felt himself shoved forward and through a door, the cool breeze hitting him in the face.

Ker struggled to escape from her captors, anger rising within her, her eyes on Brody as he has hauled across the parking lot and then pushed into the back seat of a large SUV. She froze, her feet not working for a moment, as the man holding her yanked at her arm to drag her towards the same vehicle.

Pushed down beside Brody, she glared at the three men, one sitting beside her, a cruel grin on his face as he watched her. She didn't know them, that much she knew, but she would remember them. Her memory for faces had always been excellent. She shifted closer to Brody, feeling his hand reaching for hers and tightening on it. Ker turned her head, her focus on Brody, seeing the pain that he was trying hard to hide, even as he watched the three men closely.

Ker had no idea who they were. She had not seen them before, but her father had warned her to be careful after Keefe had spoken out of turn. There had been threats coming into the office, by fax, by email, by phone, that she had just found out about. Her father hadn't told her of the packages that he and Keefe had found and turned over to the authorities.

Brody shifted his gaze from man to man, watching Ker as well, as best as he could. He didn't like that they were being driven from the town. Not one bit, he decided. Then, he began to pray, begging God to protect the lady with him, and give him the ability to save her.

The SUV was finally stopped in a density of a forested and marshy area. The door beside him was pulled open, and both he and Ker were shoved out, landing hard and awkwardly on the ground, to lie still for a moment. Brody rolled to his back, staring in disbelief as the vehicle drove away at a rapid pace, before he was on his feet, running towards the road. He slid to a stop, unbelief still on his face. He heard muttering from beside him and turned, watching Ker as she stood there, anger on her face.

"Just who were those men?" Brody's question drew her attention to him.

"I have no idea. All I know is that I am out in the boonies somewhere, it's late afternoon, and I have no idea how we are going to get home."

Brody's phone was in his hand. "I have limited service. Let me send off a text. Do you know where we are?"

Ker shrugged. "About 10 miles from town. On Old Whyte Road. Do you know the area?"

"No, I don't." He pocketed his phone, his hand reaching for hers. "Let me help you."

She shrugged away from him, heading back down the road. "I can do it myself, thank you very much."

Brody stared after her before he ran to catch up. This will be interesting, he thought. I am not sure what they wanted, but my head is aching like crazy, Lord. I

have a miles-long walk and a lady with me who doesn't
want any help.

Chapter 2

Brody finally reached out to stop Ker's forward progress, needing to rest for a moment, and thinking that she did as well.

"Again, Ker? Do you know those men?"

"No. I don't." She bit at her lip for a moment. "Dad didn't want to tell me, but Keefe let something slip. There have been threats against our company."

"And you are just telling me now? Ker!"

"What? What can you do? You're not involved." She refused to look at him.

"Not involved?" Brody stared at her, shock on his face. "Not involved? Just what do you call the lump on the back of my head and the headache that I have? Isn't that being involved?"

She glared at him, anger burning through her. "I don't want you here. Go away." She's turned and stomped away from him. Her white long-sleeved blouse was no longer the pristine colour that it had been that morning, with a rip across one sleeve where she had caught it on a wayward branch. Her black pencil skirt was dirty and stained. She limped, not willing to take off her shoes, and not willing to admit that her feet were hurting and hurting badly.

Brody stared after her, a hand on his head, before he called after her. "Ker. You're limping. What did you do to your shoes?"

Ker spun, stomping back towards him. "You have dragged me all over this forsaken area. Through bush and shrub and I don't know what all to call it. A short cut, you said. I didn't see any short cut. And during that time, a heel came off my shoe. What do you expect me to do? Walk around on who knows what in bare feet?"

"Ker! Stop! I didn't know that. You should have told me."

"Told you?" Her voice rose in anger. "And just what would you have done? Left me there?" Her hands reached to yank off her shoes, and she pitched them at him. "Here. You take them. You walk in them." She turned and almost ran from him.

Brody caught the shoes that she threw at him, staring at them before he stared after her. Running after her, his hand on her arm stopped her.

"Ker? Please? Don't walk that way. You're going the wrong way."

"And just how would you know that? You told me that you didn't know the area." Her words were bit out, almost needlelike in their delivery.

Neither one of them heard the truck slowly approaching them, nor heard it pull to a stop not far from them. Brandon and Benen, friends of Brody's, exchanged a glance, grins on their faces, as they watched their friend from the safety of Brandon's truck.

"I think that Brody has a live one there." Brandon continued to grin.

"I think he does. Ouch!" Benen winced. "Did she just throw her shoes at him?"

Brandon laughed. "I think that she did. Should we rescue him?"

Benen shrugged. "I suppose that we must. After all, he did send us a text message, didn't he? I wonder why he's out here, though."

Brody finally turned, hearing the truck approaching him once more. "Ker. There are friends. We can leave."

"You can leave. I'm not going anywhere." Ker was being stubborn, but the fear and panic that was rising within her drove her anger.

"Yes, you are. We are not leaving you out here." Brody waited. "Ker? Let's move." When she still stood, a mutinous look on her face, refusing to move, he simply reached for her arm and pulled her to the truck.

Standing with the door to the back seat open, Brody waited for Ker to jump up on the seat.

"Ker? Let's go."

"No. Absolutely not! I am not getting into another vehicle with you. I don't know these people."

"Ker. In the truck, now!" Brody waited, finally tossing her shoes on the floor, picking her up and seating her, pulling the seatbelt around her.

"How dare you!" Ker spat her words at him.

"I dare because you need to be in here! I dare because I am tired, my head is hurting, and I need to get it looked at! I dare because someone is out there watching us, waiting for night to fall so that he can kidnap you again! Is that enough?" Brody's anger had flared, and his words were like barbs directed at her.

Brandon and Benen exchanged a glance, their amusement barely contained.

"Ready to go home, Brody? And maybe you would like to introduce us to your lady?" Brandon's voice rippled with his laughter.

"Shut up, Brandon. And you too, Benen. This has not been a good day!"

"We can see that." Benen shifted to watch them, noting that the lady had refused to look at any of them. "Hello. I'm Benen, and this is Brandon. We're friends of the man back there who seems to have mishandled you."

Ker stared at him, unable to believe that she had heard what he had said.

"Benen, shut up. It's been bad enough already today without you starting. How does Cadee put up with you?" Brody sighed, suddenly weary, his head beginning to pound heavily. "I'm sorry. I didn't mean that."

"I know. You're just frustrated and in pain. And we can see why." Benen turned back around, his laughter filling the cab, Brandon barely containing his. "And Cadee puts up with me because we love each other."

Brody just shook his head, hearing the snicker that came from Brandon.

"Do you say these were friends of yours?" Ker's finger stabbed towards each one. "What friend says that?"

"Draw in the claws, kitten. We've been friends for many years. We've also been through too much together to bear any grudges." Brody twisted to watch behind him. "Did you see any vehicles waiting?"

"No, we didn't. And we would like to hear what happened to you." Brandon glanced in the rearview mirror to find Ker staring at Brody and nodded. She's the one, isn't she, Lord? She's his lady. Another adventure. "And by the way, didn't we tell Brennen that nine was enough?"

"Shut up, Brandon. Just get us home."

Brandon's comment and Brody's response had Ker staring at Brody once more, a puzzled look in her eyes. She really was not sure what she had landed into. She never talked to friends that way, nor did her brother. Her mother would not have allowed it.

Benen had looked down at his phone as it chimed and then spun around. "You're Ker Deeks?"

"I am. What do you want to do about that?" Ker was scared, and for Ker to be scared, her anger flared.

—

"Because Barnabas just sent word that your home has burnt, there has been a bomb threat at your office, and Brody's truck is still there at your father's business. They're looking for you two."

"Tell Barnabas that so far, we're okay. We'll talk when we get back." Brody stared out the side window, not seeing the looks that Ker kept throwing his way.

"Barnabas said to bring Ker with you. He'll settle her into one of the suites for the night. Her father and mother are heading our way."

"That's good."

Ker stared at the three men. "Don't I get a say in where I go?"

"No!" The three men spoke as one.

Chapter 3

Pulling to a stop in front of the Barnabas Foundation building that they all called home, Brandon shifted to study Brody. He frowned. Brody is hurting, Lord, and I don't know why. All we got was that cryptic text, asking someone to come and pick him up and then where he was. He shared a look with Benen, who shook his head.

Ker stared up at the building as best she could from inside the truck, finally remembering to snap her mouth closed. She had heard of the Foundation, knew her father was friends with the founder but had never been here. The three-story building was a mixture of dark brown brick and dark brown board and batten siding, with balconies for each suite.

Brody roused, his eyes narrowed from pain, before he reached for the door handle, to shove the door open and then slid down, the slight jar of landing on the pavement causing his head to pound even more. Benen was out of the truck and around to stand beside him, waiting for him to ask for help.

"Brody?"

"It's okay, Benen. Doc's around, isn't he?"

"He should be. Brady's not. He's on shift tonight."

"That's what I thought." Brody turned to Ker, finding her watching him closely. "Come on, kitten. Let's get you inside. My friends will help you out."

She shook her head. "No way, buster. I am not going into that building. I have had enough for the day."

"Ker, you don't have a choice. The police have asked that you be kept safe here. If necessary, they will arrest you." Brody hated to be stern with her, but she was not leaving him much of a choice. When she still refused to move, he simply reached into the truck, undid her seatbelt, slid her towards him, and gathered her into his arms.

Ker was shocked, to say the least, that Brody simply picked her up and walked towards the building. She began to struggle.

"Let me down. I can walk,"

"On those feet? I don't think so." Brody nodded at Benen as he held the door open for him, not paying attention to some of his friends and their ladies, gathered in the lobby seating area, who stared at him, some open-mouthed.

"Put me down, buster." Ker's fear was driving her anger.

"Ker, enough. I'll let you down once we get to Doc's apartment. He's an Emergency room physician. He'll need to assess both of us."

"You, maybe. I'm okay."

"Really?" Brody stared down at her, seeing how the day had fatigued her, leaving dark shadows under her beautiful eyes, and loosening the curls from the ponytail that she had put her hair in that morning. "I would say otherwise."

Abruptly dropped to her feet, Ker bit her lip, realizing that Brody had been right, after all. And she hated that. Keefe was always trying to get the best of her, and she refused to let him or any male do that to her. She stared down at her hand, caught tight in Brody's strong grasp, and for once didn't try to move away from him. She refused to let anyone touch her or hold her hand, she thought, and here this man had carried her and was now holding her hand. She paled as she realized that she had let him do that very deed earlier in the day.

Benen waved as he walked away, amusement still in his eyes, looking for Cadee. Her parents ran the local homeless shelter, and Cadee was always gathering new clothes to take in. He figured that Ker would need some, even if she really didn't welcome them.

Lord, what is with her? Brody is trying to keep her safe and alive, is what I'm thinking, but she just doesn't seem to want his help. Cadee simply stood and stared at him as he explained what was going on with Brody.

"Brody? And a lady? Of course, I have some clothes that should work." Cadee spun away from Benen before she was back in his arms. "Thank you, Benen, for not teasing him too much."

"And who said that I did that?" Benen stood, a grin on his face, watching as she quickly sorted through the piles of clothing on the spare room bed.

Cadee shook a finger at him. "I know you, Benen. I know how you fellows are. You tease and torment one another."

Barnabas stood for a moment, watching as Brody and Ker disappeared into the elevator. A frown covered his face. He had spoken with his father and been informed that Ker would need to be kept safe, that threats had been levelled at the private investigations firm her father operated, and that she was a target. He sighed. Another one, Lord? When does it end? And I would say that Brody is involved.

Doc stood in his kitchen doorway, watching as Brody carefully moved towards him, his grip not easing on Ker's hand.

"Brody? What did you go and do, son?" Doc pointed to a chair, a frown on his face at how slowly Brody was walking.

"Got knocked over the head, Doc. It hurts. And the headache is bad." He shoved Ker down in a chair, bending carefully to lift her feet to another chair, shocking her at that. "This is Ker Deeks. We've had to do quite a trek and she had on high-heeled shoes. It was not our choice that this happened. It was through brush and a marshy area. She also lost a heel to her shoe."

"She did, did she? Hello, Ker. I'm Doc and this is my wife, Anna. Let's have a look at you two." Doc nodded as Anna moved around, finding juice for the two, knowing they needed something sweet. "Brody, you have quite a lump there."

"I know." Brody grimaced and then groaned. "I never saw it coming."

"You fellows usually don't. Ker, I'll let you go with Anna. Get yourself cleaned up." Doc looked around as a tap came to the door, and Cadee entered. "Cadee? What are you doing here?"

"Benen was one of the ones who rescued Brody. He asked if I had some new clothes that I was waiting to take in." She held up a pile and smiled at Ker. "Hi. I'm Cadee. I understand that you met my husband, Benen, earlier. Pay him no mind. He loves to tease and torment."

Ker stared at her, not quite sure if she was telling the truth or no. "Hi."

"Here. Benen asked that I bring you these. They are all brand new. Just take your pick." As Ker went to refuse, Cadee shook her head. "No, it's okay. We take in donations for the shelter Mom and Dad run. No one knew these were even coming." She hugged Brody and then was gone, leaving Ker staring after her and then at the three in the room with her.

Chapter 4

Early the next morning, Brody tapped at Doc's door, waiting for him to answer. His sleep had been fragmented at best, even with the pain medications that Doc had insisted he take. He was concerned for Ker and just wanted to make sure that she was still there and okay.

Doc stood for a moment, a hand on the door, amusement in his eyes that he quickly hid. Brody was acting just like the others, he thought. The fine young men fall quickly and at first sight for their ladies, or most of them did.

"Brody? So nice of you to drop by and visit us. Come in. I have coffee on."

Brody stared at him for a moment, before he caught the twinkle in Doc's eyes. "Gee, thanks, Doc. I could use a cup of your coffee and your company. We haven't talked in a day or so."

Doc began to shake with his laughter. "Got me there, young man. Here, sit. Anna was up and out early. Something about a breakfast meeting that she had to attend. She did leave her breakfast casserole for us."

"Sounds good." Brody sat, his head in his hands, wishing the drummers would stop their music.

"How are you feeling this morning, Brody?" When Brody just sat, not responding, Doc sighed. "About like that, eh? We'll see what we can do about

---

it." He turned to study the hallway, not hearing Ker moving around yet. "Your young lady isn't up yet. Anna checked on her as she was leaving."

"Was she up in the night?"

"No. Neither of us heard her. She was done in, Brody, as they say. What did you go and do?"

"I have no idea, Doc. At the wrong place at the wrong time, I guess." Brody sipped at his coffee, his mind trying to sort everything out. Lord, I see Your hand in this. I just don't know where it's going.

"No, Brody. At the right place at the right time. Who knows where Ker would have ended up if you hadn't been there."

Ker heard the men talking and hesitated just outside the doorway. She had arisen somewhat earlier, spent her time in her devotions as she always did, glad that a Bible was on the bedside table. She had then stood, her fingers touching the clothing that Cadee had left for her. She had lingered on a pair of beautiful leggings, the jade and cream and peach drawing her in. Her favourite colours, she thought. She had never worn leggings, had always thought that she couldn't. She had known her parents' feelings on them and realized that she had let them sway her from her own decision.

Her decision made, she had quickly dressed, finding a long turtleneck tunic with three-quarter sleeves in a soft cream. She smiled. Yes, she thought. It was time she started making her own decisions. If that meant that she had to set sail on a new career and make a break with her father's company, then she would. She drew on heavy socks, finding her feet cold and still sore. Doc had dressed the cuts and bruises and blisters, not saying much. That had surprised her. If it had been her own family doctor, she would have received a lecture, that she knew.

Brody caught a slight movement in the hall and then was on his feet, moving towards her, his hands outstretched without thinking. Ker studied his face, studied his hands, and then reached for them, finding his grasp warm and welcoming.

"How did you sleep, Kitten?" His voice was low, making sure that only she could hear him.

She heard Doc rattling away in the kitchen and wondered if he was doing that on purpose. She looked up at Brody, finding his attention on her, and not on what was going on behind him.

"Okay, I guess. I was tired. And my feet still hurt."

"They will. Here, let's get you to a seat. Doc said Anna left us breakfast." Brody drew her into the kitchen and to a seat, waiting for her to decide what she wanted in a tea.

"Brody? Your head? Is it any better?" Ker glanced up quickly, disquieted to find him watching her intently.

"Not really." He held up a hand as she went to protest. "It's okay, Ker. I'm just glad I was there. I hate to think of what might have happened to you." He looked around as he heard the door open and close. "We're going to need to speak with the police."

—

"Yeah, right. About that." Ker studied her hands, not willing to look up. "They will never believe me. I know that."

"And why not?"

"Just because. They have never believed the ladies in town."

Barnabas and Bruce had entered the kitchen quietly, listening to the conversation before they exchanged a glance. Bruce was puzzled. He knew of Ker, but not that this was her opinion of her town's police. Barnabas merely shook his head, took the plate of food held out to him, and sat beside Ker.

Brody nodded at the two men but kept his attention on Ker. He frowned for a moment, seeing the conflicting emotions flitting across her face.

"Ker? Talk to me. What happened yesterday? It's more than just nothing. And we do have to talk to the police and give our statements."

Ker drew a deep breath, a sober look on her face. "I know we do." Her voice was barely a whisper. "But I can't. Not to them."

"Okay. So, I have a detective friend. He could come out and take the statements. He's been through a lot with us over the last couple of years."

She shrugged, finally looking up at him. "Brody? Why? Why did this happen?"

Chapter 5

Bruce began to pray, causing Ker to jump and stare at them. She had not heard them come in, so focused was she on Brody. That's not good, she thought. I could have disappeared again.

Looking up at last, Bruce picked up his fork and then pointed it at Ker's plate. "Eat, young lady. Then, we'll talk. And yes, Brody, I have spoken to Will. He's sending Dallas out. He hasn't said but he seems to give the impression that he shares Ker's opinion of some of her police force."

"He does? Who's he?" Ker looked between the four men.

"He's our chief of police, Kitten." Brody chewed his mouthful of food and then swallowed. "He's also a good friend of ours, and a member of our church."

"Oh!" They could see Ker relaxing. "That's good. I don't know that any of our force even goes to church."

An hour later, Dallas tapped the papers of their statements together and set them into his briefcase. He was puzzled. What happened didn't make sense.

"Ker? What else can you tell me? This is puzzling."

"I know. Keefe let slip that there had been threats against our business. He didn't say that they had been directed at me." She paled. "Why?"

"Talk to us, Ker. Tell us exactly what it is your father does. I can guarantee, it goes no further. Not unless we have to do that, and that is only with your permission." Barnabas leaned forward, his pen in his hand.

"It won't? Okay. Dad is a private investigator. He searches for missing and exploited children and teens. It is dangerous, that I know. He has a team that works with the authorities wherever he tracks down the children. He never goes in on his own or sends his team in. He leaves that to the ones who are trained in that."

"Okay. So has anything happened recently that would make someone come after you? And how well known is it what your father does?"

"Dad flies undercover, as he says. He works by word of mouth. There is a network out there that has the names of those willing to help find these children. Even our building and the business name gives nothing away. But someone has to have learned what we do. Keefe did tell me that there had been an incident six months ago, I think it was. Dad has found a child, told the authorities where the child was. They refused to believe him and didn't go in. That child died. The inquest stated that if the child had been found even two days earlier, that child would have survived."

Brody nodded. It was what he had suspected, his mind searching all the scenarios that he could imagine during the night.

—

"And your father was blamed. Someone has to have told someone."

"That's what we think. Dad did have to testify, but it was a closed court. No one should have known he was there."

"Someone saw him, put two and two together, and then tracked him down." Bruce sat back, frustrated. "We'll need to talk with your parents and Keefe. Make sure they take extra care."

"Good luck with that." Ker's growing bitterness showed.

Brody just reached out and hugged her, finding her struggling at first before she relaxed against him. *What is going on, Lord? What has she been through that has caused her to react like this?*

Dallas stood, Barnabas walking him out, shutting the apartment door behind him.

"What's your reading on the situation, Dallas?" Barnabas was puzzled as well.

"She's scared, Barnabas. And my reading is that she will become angry. I talked to Benen and Brandon, and they said that she did grow angry with Brody." He rubbed a hand on his face. "I just don't get what they were after. Brody said the men never spoke, never asked for anything, just took them out and dumped them."

"I know. That doesn't make a lot of sense. Unless it was a threat directed towards her father. Dad knows him but hasn't said much about him. I don't know that he has seen him much in the last few years. Dad gathers friends and acquaintances."

"Like someone else I know." Dallas grinned and waved, walking away.

Barnabas stood for a moment, watching him, before he shook his head. Footsteps stopped beside him and he turned. Breck, his good friend and the one just under him in the work of the Foundation building, stood there.

"What's this I hear about Brody? I was away yesterday, just got in."

"Brody is off on an adventure, I would say." Barnabas brought him up to where they stood at the present time with the situation.

"Ker Deeks? I know her. I met her just recently at a church event. Brody and Ker? Now that is one couple I wouldn't have seen."

"Would we with any of them?" Barnabas stood for a moment, lost in thought. "I'm off, Breck. I have meetings that I can't miss."

"They're with Doc and Anna? Go on then, my friend. I'll pop in and see what I can find out."

Breck stood where he couldn't be seen, watching Brody and Ker. What is it, Lord, with our fellows? The lady has to be in danger before they find their life mates, the ones who You have chosen for each one.

Chapter 6

Brody slumped down in the corner of Doc's sofa, his head cushioned against a pillow that Anna had tucked under it. He was asleep, his body unable to stay awake any longer. Pain lined his face and dark shadows lined under his eyes.

Doc stood and watched him, wondering how long it would be before he could actually talk Brody into going for an X-Ray. He doubted that he could. His eyes dropped to Ker, and he smiled. She was quiet, he thought, but there was a desperation and anger in her that he seldom saw. Brody, you have your hands full.

Ker's head was on a pillow on Brody's knee, his arm cradled around it, as she too slept. His other arm cradled her body, holding her to him, her hand tight in his. She had not thought twice about lying down as she was, too tired and sore to even worry about it. She had had to admit to herself that her sleep of late had been troubled and worrisome, the nightmares driving her awake. She had not been able to pace as she would have liked to. Her mother would have been at her door, telling her to go back to bed.

She slept, this time without worries or dreams. Her grip on Brody's hand and the way that he cradled her so carefully to him brought reassurance to her that someone cared, that they would take care of her.

Doc turned as he heard a tap at his door, watching as Anna opened it, greeting Bruce and

—

33

Barnabas and then stepping back as they entered, another couple with them. Ker's parents, Doc surmised. He sighed. Somehow, he just knew, didn't he, Lord, that things would not go well. Ker had not said, but he gathered from what she didn't say that she had not been allowed to make many decisions on her own.

Introduced to Keene and Kelly Deeks, Doc pointed to the kitchen.

"In there, I think. Brody and Ker are asleep in the living room and I won't disturb."

"Just what do you mean?" Kelly Deeks was instantly hostile. "That's not right. Let me find my daughter." She moved past him, standing and staring at her daughter, before an angry sound came from her and she moved to enter the room.

Doc took one look at her, clapped his hand over her mouth, and bodily carried her from the apartment and down the hall where he set her back down on her feet, removing his hand.

"How dare you! How dare you touch me! Let me by!" Kelly found that she could not bluff Doc, or make him move. "Out of my way!"

"No, you're not going back into my apartment. Not with that attitude." Doc had dealt with too many unruly patients to step aside. He could see some of the men from the building heading their way, grim looks on their faces. Word had gotten around that Brody had been hurt and that he was at Doc's, along with the lady everyone was surmising was his.

———

"I most certainly can. That's my daughter in there." Kelly tried her best to move past him, not seeing Keane and Bruce standing watching them. Barnabas had stayed at the apartment, standing guard at the door.

"Not in my apartment. I get to decide who is welcome there."

Kelly finally looked up, anger sparking from her eyes. "We'll see about that. Bruce, make him move."

"Sorry, Kelly. He is correct. It is his home. I don't make those decisions for him." Bruce watched her closely. "As for Ker, she is an adult. She can make her own decision as to where she wants to be and who she wants to be with. It's time that happened."

Keane drew in a deep breath, knowing that Bruce had just hit at Kelly where she grew the most angriest. She did not tolerate anyone telling her what to do with her children, not even her children themselves.

"Kelly, enough. Let's go." Keane reached for her arm, having her jerk it away from him.

"I'm not done. I'm not leaving until I remove Ker from there."

"It's not happening, Kelly." Bruce nodded at Keane and they both grasped one of her arms, leading her away, directly towards the men of the building who had gathered. Brady, the paramedic, still in his uniform, followed them, Breck on his heels.

"Breck? What's going on? I was just coming in when I heard the shouting."

"You were on duty, I gather yesterday?" At Brady's nod, Breck continued. "Brody had gone out on an assignment, ending up dumped in the woods somewhere with the owner's daughter. He's likely got a concussion. She was trying to walk back in high-heeled shoes. Brandon and Benen went to find them and brought them here." Breck nodded towards the car waiting outside the door of the building, watching as Kelly was shoved inside, Bruce and Doc standing in such a way that she was not able to open her door and return to the building.

"I know of them. He runs an investigations firm. His daughter works for him."

"I would say that she did. I doubt that she'll go back. Brody will have something to say about that." Breck smiled at Brady's quick grin. "Yeah, he's one of you. On his adventure. I'm not sure what brought this one."

"She found Brody asleep in Doc's apartment, Ker's cuddled up to him. She took offense at that." Barnabas spoke from beside the two men. "We'll have to deal with this aftermath. I doubt Ker will want to return home."

"Let's pray that she doesn't. If that's what her life has been like, we need to rescue her." Brendon spoke from Brady's other side. "Sorry. Brody will have to rescue her."

"And he'll drag us all along on his adventure. You other nine have done that." Buckley, the minister in the group, grinned at Brady and Brendon.

"Yeah, there's that. I would not want to face her. What drives people to be that angry?" Bradon spoke up.

"Loss of control for one." Burnie, the author, had used similar ploys in his novels. "I fear for Brody and his Ker."

Chapter 7

Moving restlessly, Brody awoke, finding Breck setting down a mug of coffee on the table beside him.

"Thanks, Breck. What time is it?"

"Almost one. Doc said not to wake you. He's off for his shift."

"That late? I didn't think I would sleep." Brody rubbed at his face, his eyes on Ker as she still slept. "Ker hasn't woken up?"

"No, and it's a wonder that the two of you didn't, with the commotion earlier." Breck sat, his own mug of coffee in his hand.

"What are you talking about?"

"Ker's mother. Her parents showed up, she took offense at the two of you in here, and was adamant that she was going to awaken Ker. Doc took care of her." Breck gave a low laugh.

"He did? Moved er out of here, did he?" Brody gave a quick smile.

"He did. Carried her out of here, Barnabas said, and set her down in the hall. Her husband and Bruce finally moved her out and to Keane's car." Breck shook his head, sobering. "We're not done with her. I fear for your lady."

"I know. She hasn't said much, but I sort of got the impression that there was not a good relationship there." Brody sighed. "Not like it was with my sister and our mom and dad. We all got along, had our differences, but worked through them. I miss them."

"I'm sure that you did. You said once that the bodies had never been found."

"No, they were. They were heading home on the snowmobiles, coming across a lake that should have been frozen solid. They seemed to have hit a pressure crack, and then open water. The lake is too deep and murky for anyone to risk their lives. I was only fifteen at the time." Brody blinked rapidly. To have lost his whole family like that still troubled him.

Ker roused in turn, sitting up, and pushing her hair back from her face, frowning. Why was her hair loose, she wondered? She looked around, startled to find that she and Brody were no longer alone in the room. His arm kept her close to him, bringing comfort to her.

"Hi. I'm Breck. And you are Ker." Breck grinned at her.

Ker stared at him before looking back up at Brody. "Brody? What happened?"

"You had a much-needed rest, Kitten. So did I." Brody nodded at Breck. "This is another of my friends, but he is also just under Barnabas in the chain of command here."

Breck continued to grin at her. "That I am. Welcome to the family."

She frowned at him again. "Welcome to the family? Just what are you talking about?"

"Your mother was here." Brody's arm tightened around her as she jumped and then tied to stand up. "It's okay. Doc dealt with her. She's not here now."

"She's not? That can't be right. She would never walk away, not if she saw us."

"She saw you, Doc dealt with her as he would an unruly family member in Emergency, and Bruce and your father moved her out of the building. It was quite the sight to see." Breck just continued to grin at her. "She wasn't hurt, but you would have been. How much hurt has she done over time to you?"

Ker withdrew slightly into herself. "You don't understand. She won't let this alone. Brody, what did we do?"

"We did nothing. Doc and Anna were with us the whole time. After yesterday, we needed to be together, just to heal. And sleep is part of that." Brody's heart broke for his lady, as he began to pray for her.

"But you don't get it. Brody! You don't know her!" Ker was becoming more and more agitated.

The two men exchanged glances, not quite sure what was going on, before Brody simply bowed his head and began to pray, asking for peace for his lady, wisdom in the situation, and a swift resolution to whatever it was that Ker was facing.

Ker felt herself relaxing against Brody, feeling content, at peace, and loved. How that was, she couldn't figure out, but his character was coming through to her, and she didn't want to move from his side. She had never had that in her life, not even with her parents or brother.

Breck pulled out his phone when Brody finished, a frown on his face as he read the text message.

"This is not good, Brody. Bruce says Kelly is still on the warpath as he puts it. She is adamant that Ker is leaving here, today, and that you won't have any contact with her. If either of you refuses, she will have you charged with kidnapping, Brody."

"She will too, Brody. Oh, what will I do?" Ker fought her emotions, but for once, her tears got the better of her.

Brody simply turned her into his shoulder, taking the burden from her, seeking to bring her comfort, all the while his mind racing as to what they could do.

"Brody? There is one way out of this." Breck was hesitant to name it, but Brody nodded, knowing exactly what he was thinking.

"Marry her." Ker raised her head at that, staring at him as he repeated his words. "I marry her, Kelly can't touch her or me. If Ker agrees of her own free will and seeing that she is an adult, there is not a lot that they can do."

"You would do that?" Ker's question was soft, barely audible.

"I would, Kitten. I would do that, just for you. You need this." Brody dropped a kiss on her forehead. "We'll pray about it. Breck here will pray for us now, knowing Breck."

"That I will. And if you do decide to do this, be quick. Bruce said that she's trying to find an officer to come in and arrest you."

"She is, is she? She can try." Brody's face and voice were grim.

Chapter 8

Standing in the building chapel doorway late that afternoon, Brody stared down at Ker, her hand tight in his. They had prayed, discussed it, and then agreed. Ker hadn't shared with him, not yet, the relief that she felt, knowing he was taking on her fight for her, a fight that she hadn't known either that she was in. She looked up at him, a puzzled look in her eyes at the look in his.

"You are sure, Kitten?" Brody's voice was low.

"I am. But this is asking so much of you, Brody." Ker was troubled.

"I want to, Kitten. I truly do. For one thing, I can't walk away from you. Not now. Not ever." He nodded towards where Buckley stood waiting, his friends and their ladies in the pews, turned to watch them. Brody knew that the security in the building had been tightened for the next few days.

"Mom will try to get it set aside."

"She can try, but she had the Barnabas Foundation to go against. She won't win."

"I guess. But I don't understand."

"We'll talk later, Ker. But just understand that now that you are becoming a member of the Foundation family, you are part of a group that takes care of one another."

"Oh! I guess that we do need to talk." She walked forward on unsteady feet as he drew her to the front.

Later, Ker stood hesitantly in the conference room, not quite sure where to go. She felt like running, but the only way that she wanted to run was towards Brody. Right now, though, he was speaking with some friends, standing just a few feet away from her, his eyes on her. Cadee watched Ker closely before she approached.

"Ker? Welcome to the family. May I hug you?"

Ker spun, startled. "I guess. I've never been one for hugging."

"That's okay. We hug here, a lot. Just tell us if you're not comfortable with that and we won't. I have a friend who can't hug because of health reasons. She gives virtual hugs instead. We could do that." Cadee's face was alight with laughter.

"No, it's okay. I'm needing to make a change." Ker looked around. "I didn't realize there were so many here."

"There are. There are fourteen of the fellows. Nine, sorry, ten of them are now married. Berneen's brother is here. That's Darbie. And Hagen's twin sisters, Hailey and Hollie, are around. They have Hagen's twins with them."

"Twins? Oh, my! That's a handful."

Hagen laughed from beside her. "Both sets are. But the girls are good. We had been on our own for a bit before Brandon and I married. I understand that he gave you a bit of a hard time the other day."

<hr>

44

"That was your husband? I'm sorry. I don't think that I was too nice to either one of them."

"Hey, they are used to that. We've all given them a hard time. Still do." Fynn spoke up. "I'm married to Brady, by the way. I'll get you a flow chart of who's who. That will help."

"A flow chart? I'm sorry. I don't think that I understand." Ker was bewildered at the laughter that sprang up.

"We're not laughing at you, Ker. Fynn is known for her flow charts. She's an entomologist and before she moved here, was working in the medical examiner's office."

"You were? Fascinating. I would like to talk to you about that." Ker's interest was piqued.

Brody watched her closely, seeing her opening up to the ladies.

"She's making steps to get to know the ladies, Brody." Blair spoke from beside him.

"She is. It is going to be hard for her. She hasn't said much, but I would like to have a long talk with her mother."

"You and the rest of us. We saw what happened this morning with Doc. She's brutal." Blair shook his head.

"I heard it was bad. I didn't realize it was that bad."

"Trust me, it was. If it had been anyone other than Doc, Ker would not be standing here with you."

—

"Okay. That's good to know." Brody bit his lip as he looked around. "Listen, can you do something for me, you and the others? Can you do some research on her family?"

"Already started, Brody." Bradon spoke from where he stood behind him. "You know us. If something affects one of us, it affects us all." He nodded towards Ker. "Your head is hurting, isn't it? And Ker needs a rescue. She's trying hard but she's at her limit."

"That she is. Thanks, guys." Brody walked towards Ker, an arm coming around her. "How about it, Kitten? Ready to go?"

She looked up at him, a frown on her face. "You need to explain, buster."

Brody grinned down at her. "Explain what?"

"That word that you're always calling me. Kitten. And why you keep taking the tie from my hair."

Brody shouted with laughter, causing all eyes to find them.

"Kitten? You were like a little, itty bitty kitten yesterday. All fluffed up, hissing and spitting at us. Claws out. Sorry, but you were just so cute." He smiled down at her look of outrage. "You're adorable when you are like that. I love your spirit. And the hair? You look beautiful with it down around your face."

Chapter 9

Two days later, Ker wandered the gardens on the grounds, amazed at the variety and extent of the plantings. She stopped to watch Jaxcy, she thought it was, working in the vegetable garden. She had always wanted to get her hands dirty doing just that, but she had not been allowed. Almost without thinking, she walked towards Jaxcy, who stood, a smile on her face.

"Ker? Welcome to our building garden."

"What did you call it?"

"Our building garden. I'm supposed to be in charge, but everyone works it at some point or another. We are enjoying the fresh produce." Jaxcy looked with satisfaction at the long rows.

"Oh, that's wonderful. I've wanted to do that."

"And now you can." Jaxcy was wise enough not to question Ker's wording. "I didn't get a chance to speak with you but I do welcome you to our family."

"It's a huge family."

"It is. The fellows are all orphans." Jaxcy laughed freely at Ker's expression. "That's right. All orphans. All from different provinces. Brennen and I are both from Newfoundland and Labrador. And no, we didn't know each other before we married. It's a long story."

"And one I would love to hear. Brody said the men all share initials as well."

"That they do. All the same as Barnabas. He set it up that way. He was directed by God, he states, to do just that. All of the fellows are employed by the Foundation even though they work out in the community."

"That's an odd way of doing things." Ker was puzzled.

"It is. But part of the premise of the Barnabas Foundation is to be encouragers, just like Barnabas in the Bible. This is how it's been set up. And each of the wives has their own income from the Foundation, as part of their plan to encourage the couples." She paused. "I guess you and Brody haven't talked about that."

"We have, but we didn't get very far. He still fighting headaches and sometimes he's found it hard to articulate what he wants to say." Ker was silent, her mind racing though. "Does that mean that I don't have to go back to Dad's?"

"That it does, if that's what you and Brody want. I know that you two are still young in your friendship. Marrying as you did throw as something into it that changes it." Jaxcy bit at her lip. "Brennen ended up in my town. At the time, there was a law that said if a newcomer didn't marry someone from the town, they were jailed. I stepped in to marry him, but he had been beaten soundly, all because of me. We were married a week before he really roused. We moved back here." She reached to rub at her Shetland Sheepdog's side.

———

"This is Kerry. He'll be around if you need protection, as will Bradon's Kade. Never once worry about asking for help."

"I have never felt free to do that. I just didn't realize how controlling my mother has been. Dad too, but not as much. Keefe? I'm not sure about him anymore."

Jaxcy reached to pick up a basket of produce and handed it to her. "Here. I was picking these for you and Brody. A welcome to our garden gift for you."

"Thank you." Ker blinked back tears. "You have no idea what this means. I mean, I had friends." She stopped, anger colouring her face. "And every one was handpicked by Mom. Now, what do I do?"

"Make your own. There are nine of us here. Fynn's sister-in-law is around, as is her cousin Eric's wife. We meet once a week just as the ladies of the building for Bible study and prayer. Tonight is the night. You are welcome to join us. Now that we are even numbers again, we can split up in twos. The men do that."

"They do? Oh, how wonderful. There are so many things I am seeking to know. I just didn't know that." Ker's voice died away as she eyed the woman standing in front of her, a hulking man standing beside her. "Mom, what are you and Robert doing here? My understanding is that you were banned from here."

"I have come to take you home. Robert, bring her with us."

Robert moved towards Ker, as she backed away. She could hear Kerry growling from near Jaxcy but didn't see Jaxcy frantically sending a group text to the men, asking for help. She stumbled as she moved, almost falling.

Reaching for her, Robert's hand was cruel in its grasp. She began to fight him, yelling at her mother in anger that she was married, that she no longer had to do what Kelly said.

Kelly stared at her and then waved her hand. "Married? Not really, my dear. It can be annulled very easily. If not, you could always become a widow."

Ker stared at her mother in horror. "Mom? What did you just say?" A cruel blow across her face stopped her words, as her head whipped around from the force of her mother's hand.

"Enough of that. Robert. Head for the car with her."

Ker fought harder to escape, her free hand clawing at the man's face, her feet kicking at him as best she could. He stumbled when he tripped over her foot, taking them both to the ground. A cry of pain was wrenched from Ker even as she fell, his weight trapping her underneath him.

The men who were in the building had looked up at the text message that they received, threw down whatever it was they were doing, and ran, calling for the security guard to call for the authorities.

Breck, Brendon, and Blair raced for Robert, pulling him up and off Ker, fighting to hold him, twisting his arms behind him, and taking him to his knees. Brennen raced for his wife, pushing her behind him, a quiet word of command to Kerry.

Burnie and Brendon restrained Kelly, loud questions in the air, even as Brady dropped to his knees beside Ker. Buckley was beside him, his phone out to call for help. He could tell that Brady was worried, even from a cursory look.

"Baird?"

"Her hand, for one." He winced as Ker whimpered as he touched it. "She's broken some bones." His hand touched her face lightly. "She's taken a blow to the face as well. He's a brute." Baird turned slightly to watch the struggle going on with Kelly. "Her mother?"

Jaxcy had moved closer to him. "We were talking and then they appeared. She was taking her away. She threatened to have Brody killed."

"I did no such thing." Kelly sneered at her.

Jaxcy held up her phone. "Sorry, lady. I have it on a voice recorder. You told Ker that she could end up widowed."

Dark looks covered the men's faces even as they heard the sirens shut off in the parking lot and slamming doors and then the sound of running feet as the officers approached.

Chapter 10

Throwing open his truck door and letting it slam behind him, Brody ran for the door to the Emergency Department. Breck had tracked him down, let him know that Ker had been hurt and that Brady was on the way in with her. His heart thundered with sudden fear. *How bad, Lord? How badly hurt is she? I don't think that I could stand it if she's hurt bad.*

Breck's hand stopped his forward motion and drew him to one side.

"Brody, wait. Doc's been looking for you. He took the liberty of putting you down as her next of kin."

"That's good. What happened? She was fine when I left two hours ago. She said she was going to explore the gardens." Brody was bewildered, fear driving cohesive thought from his mind.

"She was. She found Jaxcy and they were heading back from the garden. Her mother and a bodyguard appeared. Kelly tried to take her. Jaxcy said Ker fought the man, somehow tripped him, and ended up on the ground." Breck looked around, seeing the men and ladies circling them.

"How bad?" Brody was scared to even think.

"She was backhanded, Jaxcy said. Bruising there. But it's her hand. Brady said he felt broken bones. Doc has called in the surgeons that he needs to but he'll need to talk to you."

"Surgeons?" Brody paled, Breck's hand on his arm steadying him. "That bad?"

"It is, Brody." Doc's hand rested on his young friend's shoulder. How many times have I done this, Lord? I pray each time it's the last. "Come. I'll take you to her."

Brody didn't hesitate at all, heading directly for Ker, his eyes on her face. He grew angry when he saw the bruising and the cut on her lip. His hand reached to gently touch her face, finding her turning into his hand.

Ker's eyes flickered open. "Brody? You're here. I was so afraid."

"I am. I hear that you decided to have an adventure without me."

She snorted. "That's not true. I would not call this an adventure. Mom showed up with Robert and tried to make me leave." Anger sparked in her eyes. "She threatened you. She said we would annul the marriage. Or she could have me end up a widow. I have no idea what she will do."

"We'll take all the precautions that we can. I am sure that your mother and Robert have been arrested."

"I am sure that they have been. This will destroy Dad."

"Somehow, I don't think so. We need to talk, Kitten, but right now, they need to take you to have your hand fixed."

"Why? What did I do? Slug Robert?"

Brody began to laugh, picturing her doing just that. "No, but I wish I could have. You two fell and you have broken some bones in your hand."

"Oh? Does that mean the claws will be gone?" She smirked at him as he laughed before growing quiet. "Brody? Are we sure?"

"Sure? About what? Getting married? I am. You are the one that I have been waiting for. Bringing to justice those that need to be? It seems that has become our lot?" He bent to kiss her forehead and then moved back, watching as she was removed from the room.

He stood, sorrow on his face mingled with anger. Breck and Buckley exchanged glances even as they reached to lay their hands on his shoulders and pray with him.

Two hours later, Brody once more stood beside Ker, his hand resting on her cheek, his eyes on her bandaged hand, resting as it was on a pillow just to elevate it. Anger burned inside him, anger that he knew he had to release, only he didn't know how. He would need to talk to someone, he thought, before his thoughts returned to Ker and her questions.

Bradon approached him. "How is she?"

"Still sleeping. The surgeon said that she likely would for a while. They were able to repair the breaks, thank God."

"That's great. Now for her to heal. How long, did he say?"

Brody shook his head. "I didn't ask. I was just happy that they could do the repair. He'll be by in the morning before I take her home."

They spoke for a few more moments before Bradon turned to leave. "Some of us will be in the waiting room all night, Brody. Come find us if you need to talk."

"Thank you. I might. For now, this chair will do."

Ker stirred in the night, frightened for a moment at not knowing where she was. She moved her hand and bit her lip to control her groan of pain. Staring at her hand, she could feel her anger growing, praying that God would remove it. She turned slightly, pausing, watching Brody as he slept, slumped down in an uncomfortable chair, his arms tucked across his chest, his chin down. Wonder grew in her that he would stay with her. That was not what she had been trained to expect. Her eyes closed and she slept, a prayer for protection on her lips for her husband.

Chapter 11

Sighing with frustration, Ker stared down at the clean clothes that she had chosen, her shower done. She hadn't been able to wash her hair and that bothered her. She struggled as best she could before she heard Brody's voice behind her.

"Ker? Just put on your pajamas. It's okay to do that." His hand rested on her head and she heard his softly whispered prayer for her. "Even if someone drops in, they won't care."

"It's the middle of the day. I can't do that." She fought back tears of anger.

"Yes, you can. Your mother doesn't control what you do or what you wear. Is that what she did?" He waited until she gave the barest of nods. "Okay. So, I see that we have to have a discussion about things. But for now, put on your nightwear and then come out to the kitchen."

She turned slightly as she heard him leave and quickly did what he said, reaching for her dressing gown once more before she grabbed up a pair of socks. Those she would need help with, she thought. Brody turned as she entered the kitchen, reaching for the socks, kneeling in front of her to put them on her feet, her good hand resting on his shoulder. He looked up at her as he finished, finding her studying him, confusion on her face.

"Here. I know that you can't do your hair. Let me help you. I used to help my sister every once in a while. She had a habit of spraining her wrist or fingers."

"That's so sweet, Brody. My brother wouldn't help me. At least, I don't think he would." She waited until Brody had finished, seated her at the table, and then began to brush her hair. "Brody, what if he's in the same situation as I am? What if he wants to escape and can't?"

"We thought of that, Kitten. Barnabas has tracked him down and spoken with him. For now, he has Keefe stashed away somewhere that he won't say where."

"He does? But Dad is friends with his father."

"Doesn't make a difference, Kitten. Barnabas and Bruce pray about something and then do what they are led to do."

"That's a strange way to live."

"It's the only way. We are told to seek for treasures. Right now, I have the treasure I was seeking for right here in my home."

She spun to stare at him, finding her watching her, a light in his eyes that she had caught a glimpse of before. She blushed.

"Brody, what happened to Mom and Robert?"

"Your mom was released and sent home, with a court order that she cannot contact you or come with a certain distance from you. The fellows and security here know that. Our police department has a copy of

—

that. Seeing as you are now part of the Foundation family, you will be watched carefully."

"I don't like that feeling."

He grinned, even as he prepared their lunch. "It's in a good way, Kitten. They don't track you down and monitor your every move. They just watch for our vehicles, us, and make sure that we stay safe. It's how our town works." He turned, the knife that he was using to butter the bread for their sandwiches held up in the air.

"Okay. It's just strange." She looked up at him. "I'm angry about all this. Mom took so much, and I let her."

"You didn't know any different. Now that you do, you'll never let her again. I'll help to make sure of it." He sat, reaching for her hand before asking the blessing on their meal. "We'll talk, Kitten. I'm angry too, but there is something about what your Dad did that bothered me."

Ker didn't respond, not quite sure how to. She finally pushed back her plate and stood, wandering through the apartment, seeing the office that Brody had set up for himself, and then inspecting the bedrooms, before she returned to the living room and then headed for the balcony, finding a wicker rocker to sit in.

Brody stood and watched her, before he too sat in the matching wicker chair, his hand out for hers. "I love this balcony. I come out here to pray, to think, to meditate."

"It's a quiet place to do that. Brody, what did you mean about Dad's work?"

"I mean that we've been looking into it. It's not what it seems. I'm sorry, Kitten. I don't mean to put your parents down."

"I know, Brody. In the last six months or so, something changed with them. Mom became more angry and controlling. Dad didn't say anything, just let her. He was away more. What does that mean?"

"It means that the fellows will do more digging, trying to determine what has happened. To try and find out where the problems started." He tightened his grip on her hand. "And for you, it means that you heal. Not just physically. You have a lot of healing to do. And I am thankful God chose me to help you do just that."

A week later, Ker stood beside Cadee and Berneen in the lobby, watching as the men searched outside the area. Ker had received a text from her mother, threatening her. When it was traced, the signal came from the Foundation property. She was afraid but also angry. She couldn't see Brody and knew that he would be a target of her mother, her mother not liking being thwarted in her plans.

"Ker? Come. Let's sit." Berneen's arm around her drew her to a chair in the lobby. "Let's pray."

"I can't, Berneen. I am just so angry."

"We get that, Ker. We really do. We can still pray for you, and for the anger to leave." Cadee looked up as some of the other ladies approached.

"I know. I guess that I'm just not sure that I want to let it go. And I have to." Ker sighed, not sure how to word what she wanted to say.

"We get that, Ker." Hagen smiled at her. "We all went through anger when we had what we term as our adventures.

Brody turned as he heard a sound from behind him, ducking the fist heading for him. His own fist drove upwards and into the man's jaw, dropping him to the ground. Brody pulled the man's belt from him and tied his hands behind him, waving at Bradon as he approached.

"Is he the only one?"

"I don't think so. Security picked up on at least two on the cameras near the building." Bradon touched Kade's neck. "Okay, boy. Let's search." Kade gave a low woof and moved off, his hackles rising.

"He's found a trail."

"That he has." Bradon sent off a quick text. "Dallas is on his way out. He was anyway. He needs to talk to you two."

"Doesn't he always?" Brody paused, his eyes on Kade. "What's he doing?"

"He's found someone. That's his signal." Both men had kept their voices low. "Wait here, Brody. I'm going forward. I'll be back."

Brody waited, not liking the feeling that he was getting. He crept forward, suddenly not wanting to be on his own.

"Brody?"

"Bradon? What did you find?" Brody stared at the man lying in front of them.

"He was out when I got here. That's what was throwing Kade off."

"Who?"

"That I would like to find out. He's on our side, I would think." Bradon stood, his hand on Kade's head. "Okay, boy. Release." Kade relaxed, leaning into Bradon.

Ker's head was still down as the men returned to the lobby, the security guard unlocking the doors. She didn't hear the murmurs from the ladies or see Brody walking towards her. She jumped as she felt arms around her, her head whipping around to stare at Brody.

"Brody? I was so worried."

"It's okay, Kitten. We have the two men that were here. Dallas is outside. He'll be in shortly to talk to us."

"I don't understand, Brody. What happened?"

"What happened is that Brody took out one man. Kade alerted to the second one but someone beat us to him." Bradon sank down, Ennis perched on the arm of his chair. "It's so strange."

"It is. Someone was out there watching us. I don't like that feeling."

"Nor do I." Barnabas had approached, the rest of the men gathering around them. "Fellows, we'll be putting in more security once more. Make sure you know who's around you at all times. Ladies, I'll leave it to your fellows to figure out what you are going to do. I know we can't lock any of you up. It wouldn't work anyway." He turned and walked towards Dallas.

"Barnabas, we need to talk, but first I need to talk to Brody and Ker." Dallas was watching the couple.

"I know you do. Just so you know, I talked to her brother. He's safe and way from here. No one knows where he is."

"Okay. Just keep him there. Word on the street is that someone is after him as well as Ker."

"That's what I had heard." Barnabas nodded towards them. "Finish up with them, and then find me. I'll throw something on the grill and we can eat. We haven't done that in a while."

"Sounds good. I'm going off the clock once I finished with them."

Chapter 13

Ker paced the apartment that night, worrying the bandages on her hand. Bradon had stepped out into the hall with Dallas, their conversation coming to her through the open door. What had Mom gone and done? She had been receiving messages from her and was just ignoring them. The anger in the content was growing. Her father had not been in touch, and that puzzled her. He always kept in touch with her, checking in three to four times a day.

"Ker? You okay?" Brody's arms came around her.

"I really don't know. I know that I am angry and I need to get rid of that. Brody? I haven't heard from Dad. Not in a couple of days." She looked up at him. "I haven't answered them. Mom keeps trying. But Dad always checks in during the day."

"I see. Dallas asked if we had seen him. They haven't been able to find him."

"Oh, no. What did she do?"

"Your mother? That's what we're looking into. The fellows are hard at work. I'll take you down to the conference room tomorrow and you can talk to them yourself."

Ker nodded. "Do you know if Keefe is okay?"

"He is. Barnabas talked to him today. No one has been around him."

"That's good." Her head went down on his shoulder and she just let him hold her, finding herself relaxing, and her anger abating. "Why do you calm me, Brody?"

"It's not me. It's God. I'm just a channel for Him to use." He dropped a kiss on her forehead. "How be you head off to bed? It's late and you're tired."

"I will. Thank you, Brody, for being who you are." She walked away, leaving him staring after her, a bemused look on his face.

Brody reached for his phone as it gave a muted ring. Dallas? He wasn't on duty and had just left.

"Dallas?"

"Brody. I'm heading back your way. Where's Ker?"

"I just sent her to bed."

"Keep her up. I need to talk to her."

Ker had returned, intent on asking Brody something, as he turned and reached out a hand for her.

"She's still up. Dallas, what is going on?"

"I'll explain when I get there. Keep your doors locked. And I mean them all, including your balcony door. Don't answer except for myself or one of the building people." Dallas' phone clicked off, leaving Brody heading to check the balcony doors.

Ker followed him, a puzzled look on her face. "Brody?"

"Dallas is on his way back. He wants us to lock ourselves in."

"But the balconies? They can't get up to them."

"Oh, but they can. Jaxcy and Brennen were kidnapped by men using the balcony."

Ker paled and then dropped to the couch. "I don't like this, Brody. You're scaring me."

He was beside her, a hand reaching for hers. "I don't mean to, Kitten. Let's pray until Dallas gets here."

Dallas tapped at their door, Barnabas and Brady with them, Buckley hurrying up to be with them. Brody stared at the four of them, concern on his face.

"Dallas? What's going on?"

"Let us in, Brody. We need to talk." Dallas' face was grim.

"We're in the living room." Brody watched as his friends seated themselves, Buckley raising a hand to indicate he wanted to pray. When they looked up, Brody's attention was on Dallas. "Dallas?"

"Brody. Ker. Have you heard from your father in the last few days?"

She shared a look with Brody. "No, I haven't and that's unusual. Not that I was answering his texts or voice mails. Why?"

"Because we found his car. It had been dumped near where you two were. It was burnt." Dallas' hand went up at her exclamation of shock. "No, he wasn't in it. We searching but with night coming on, it is tricky. We'll be taking in dogs in the morning. And that area is in our jurisdiction, just in case you wondered."

"It is? Then, you can investigate what happened to us?" Ker was puzzled. "I still don't get it."

"None of us do. We're working through what we know. We'll get it sorted out."

"But at what cost? I know enough to know someone will be seriously hurt or even killed. Mom threatened Brody with that."

"We know, Ker." Buckley's voice broke in. "What Dallas needs, I think, from you is a list of anyone that your father had problems with, no matter how small or minor it seems."

"Why do you ask?" Ker felt Brody's hand tightening on hers.

"We need to know if you have any idea of someone who would want to harm him. We need to track his last movements." Dallas frowned down at his notes. "Did you hear from him yesterday?"

"No, not since the day we married." Ker sank back against the couch. "What did she do?"

"What did who do?" Barnabas had a good idea of who she meant.

"Mom? What did she do?"

Chapter 14

Dallas stared at her, puzzled for a moment, before he caught the look on Brody's face and then nodded. *He suspects something, doesn't he? Lord, I am getting tired of this. Fighting for my friends. Having them hurt, almost killed. Their ladies worried and hurt as well. How many more months and years can I do this?*

"Explain, please, Ker, if you will." Barnabas spoke up, Brady watching him intently.

"I'm not sure that I can. I'm sorry. Right now, I am so angry with her. She's damaged me without me being aware of that." Brody's hand tightened on hers again. "I am not aware of anyone who would want Dad hurt, or that he had run-ins with. I wasn't privy to that information. If there were any issues, they were never discussed in front of me. Keefe might know more than I did. Mom kept a tight control over what I did at the office, who I saw and when." She turned to look at Brody. "That's why I was surprised with Dad asked me to meet with you. He had never in the past."

"Do you think, then, it was planned for you to be on your own when the men came in?" Dallas shared a look with Brody.

Ker shrugged. "I have no idea. Dad had set up the appointment. Then, that morning, he just told me I was to meet with the new paralegal that was coming in. I was to go over the forms with him and find out what he would do to change them." She looked back up at Dallas. "The only one I knew that Dad had concerns about was the new lawyer in the law firm that he had dealt with for over twenty years. He wouldn't say why he all of a sudden pulled all the legal work from them."

"He did? That's something that he would not do under normal circumstances?"

Shaking her head, Ker watched Dallas closely, not seeing Buckley and Brady watching her. "No, he wouldn't. They were both adamant that they had to use that firm. I never felt comfortable around the men. I refused to go near them. In fact, I would leave the office if I knew they were coming. That was what was so unusual." She paused, thinking back over the week or so before that. "But then, Dad had not been himself for a week or so. I thought that he was worried about one of his contacts or someone that he was trying to find."

"That is possible." Dallas studied his notes. "Now, that day. I know that you have given me your statements. Have either one of you thought of anything?"

Brody spoke up. "I didn't see much, but it just seemed strange how we were just taken out there and dumped. Brandon and Benen said that they didn't see any vehicles in the area."

"And didn't you say it was in your jurisdiction? Why there?" Ker was puzzled but she was also angry. "Dallas, find these people. Find out why they did this. There has to be a reason."

"I am sure there is. We are hearing rumours on the street regarding you, Ker. I can't emphasize enough that you stay close to the building or if you are out, be aware of what is around you. Stay close to whoever it is you are with." Dallas rose, his thoughts dark. He had felt his phone vibrate and needed to take the message that he knew was waiting for him.

Brady and Barnabas walked out with him, their conversation quiet, as Dallas pulled out his phone. He sighed. He was to be off at midnight. That was not happening, not now.

"Brady, Barnabas. Make sure they stay close to someone. I need to run."

"We will." Brady watched him walk away. "I don't like that he left like that."

"No, but we have no idea why. All we can do is pray for him. And for Brody and Ker. She's seeking for freedom and peace, Brady."

"She is. I pray that she finds them. Catch you later." Brady walked away.

Barnabas hesitated and then headed for his office. He needed to talk to his father, but he knew his father was out west and not readily available for that very conversation.

Buckley had remained, talking with the couple, reading from the Testament that he pulled from his pocket, and then praying with them. He rose, his eyes on the wall in front of him, suddenly hesitant to leave, but not knowing what else to do.

"Thanks, Buckley. Your support of all of us is so appreciated." Brody walked out with him, shutting the door behind him. "I am afraid for her."

"I know that you are. I can feel that fear. She's afraid, too. What was that about her mother?"

"Her mother was or is rather controlling. Ker has been talking more and more as she finds release from that control. She is struggling with life-long emotions."

"I am sure she is. I will continue to pray. Come and find me if you need to talk."

"I will do that." Brody stood, his hand on the outside of his door, praying, before he entered, finding Ker standing waiting for him, coming readily into his open arms and welcoming his hug.

"Kitten? You okay?"

"I don't know, Brody. I just don't know. I hate this." Her voice was muffled against him.

"I know that you do. We'll make it through. I have no doubt about that. Here, head off to bed. The surgeon wants to see you tomorrow, doesn't he?"

"He does. I just don't get all this." She turned and walked away, her shoulders slumping in defeat.

Brody watched her walk away, his heart breaking for her, before he moved to clean up the mugs and whatnot from the coffee that they had shared with their friends. He walked through the apartment, checking doors and windows, turning off lights. He hesitated at Ker's bedroom before he entered, the light from the bedside lamp low. He stood, his head tilted, a sad smile on his face as he watched the tears creep down her face as she slept. He simply laid down beside her, pulling a blanket over himself, and cuddling her to him. Tonight, this was what she needed, to be held.

Chapter 15

A week later, Ker turned from studying the roses in the rose garden. She had clipped a few to take up to the apartment, needing that today. She stopped as she saw the man waiting for her.

"Who are you?" Fear drove her anger.

"I'm here for you. You need to come with me."

"I don't think so. I'm not going anywhere with you."

"Oh, but I say you are. Your mother wants to speak with you."

Ker backed away, knowing that she was near the edge of the garden, and just might be able to escape and make her way back around to the building.

"Sorry. She can't contact me."

"That paper?" The man flicked his fingers. "That's nothing. She stated that you are to come with me and now."

"Sorry. She has no control over my movements. I'm married now."

"That's what you say. She says that you aren't." The man moved towards her.

Ker dropped her roses and dove behind a bush, her breath held as she crept away from the garden and then around to the edge of the walk, not seeing the

—

man, but hearing his curses from behind her. She ran, her feet flying over the path, heading for the building, not sure if she would make it in time.

Blair had turned as he heard running footsteps and then held out his hand.

"Here, Ker. Let's get you inside. I don't like that you're running."

"Mom sent someone. He's behind me, I think."

"Okay. In you go. Head for your place."

"I will. Thank you, Blair." She ran, not waiting to see if the man had appeared.

Blair stepped back outside, his eyes searching but not seeing anyone. He frowned. Ker would not have been running like that if she hadn't been afraid. Benen appeared beside him.

"Blair?"

"Ker just ran back from the rose garden. She said her mother had sent someone to bring her to her."

"That's what we've been waiting for. Come on." Benen held up a hand. "There. Just behind the tall shrub. That's not one of us. I'll head this way. You go that way."

The strategy worked as they approached the man from either side, their hands on his arms preventing him from leaving. They directed him back to the building and to the security office. The patrol officer who responded just shook his head.

"Twister, what did you get involved in this time?"

The man, Twister his street name, simply refused to answer, knowing that if he did, he would be locked away for a long time. Maybe, he thought, if he didn't say anything, he would be out soon.

"He tried to kidnap Brody's wife. Her mother sent him. And there is a restraining order to keep her mother from contacting her." Benen spoke from behind the man.

"Is that right? Twister, it doesn't matter if you talk or not. With that, we can put you away. You're wanted for too many crimes."

Twister finally looked up, a whine in his voice as he spoke. "If I talk, what's in it for me?"

The officer just shook his head. "This time, Twister, that doesn't work. Out you go."

Benen finally tapped at Brody's door, Blair beside him. He could hear muttering as Ker approached the door.

"Ker? It's me, Blair. Benen is here as well."

She cracked open the door, only one eye visible. "I can see that. Are you sure?"

"Sure about what?" Benen grinned, having seen her sense of humour before.

"That's is just you. That no one is hiding behind you somewhere."

"Nope. It's just us. Oh! And Brody." Benen grinned at Brody as he approached. "Brody, will you ask your wife if we can come in? We've asked politely but she has refused to open the door."

"I'd refuse to open the door to you as well if I was Ker. But since I'm not and we're friends, I'll let you in." Brody grinned as he moved past them, his arms out for Ker. He had received her panicked text and headed home as soon as he explained to his employer. Ker didn't understand, he didn't think, that their employers didn't pay their wages.

"Ker, what did you do to these two?"

"Me?" Ker's voice rose in frustration. "I did nothing. It was that man."

"Man? What man?" Brody sobered instantly.

"The man who tried to take me to Mom. Does she not get it? That I want nothing to do with her." She glared at the other two men as they tried to cover their snickers. "I'm so glad that you find this funny."

Benen's grin grew. "Ker, you are so good for us all. We need that refreshing voice that you bring to the family." Then, he sobered. "Twister, as he is called, was brought in by her mother, Brody, to bring her back to her. Between Blair and I, we managed to stop him from leaving."

"Thank you. I'm glad no one was harmed."

Blair shook his head. "She doesn't give up very easily. Ker, what is it that you know?"

"I'm sorry?"

"Do you know something or someone that you're not supposed to? It seems to me that it is going well beyond just control for her." Blair tried to be polite, not saying what he really felt.

"I wish I knew. I didn't meet anyone. They kept me in the office. Any meetings were after hours." She twisted to stare up at Brody. "So, why did Dad arrange for you to come in the daytime?"

"Trying to protect you? Give you a way out of the business and the building?" Benen had been brainstorming with the others. "We've been doing some research, Ker. That research? We need to talk to you about, but some of your father's work has not been real legal."

"It hasn't? Then, that's why." Her anger flared and then died away. "Getting angry doesn't help, does it? So, what do I seek for then?"

"Peace. Understanding. A closer walk with God." Benen raised a hand as she went to protest. "I know, Ker. You're trying all that, but sometimes we try too hard. We need to just be still and let God work. Sometimes, we go through things that we won't expect. Know that we are praying for both you and Brody."

Chapter 16

Twister refused to cooperate with the investigators, frustrating Dallas, who finally just shut the door to the interrogation room and walked away. He has to know more, Dallas thought, but how do we reach him. He had been working away, bringing his notes up to date on all his cases, when a sudden commotion roused him from his computer. He was on his feet, out of his door, and heading for the cells.

"What is going on?" He stopped one of the officers running towards him.

"Someone got to Twister. He's dead."

"What? I talked to him, what an hour ago? How did that happen?"

"That's what we don't know. We pulling surveillance tapes now."

Dallas nodded. "Let me know what you find out. Right now, I have to tell a friend and his wife that the man who tried to abduct her is dead." He turned as Will Peters, the police chief, stopped beside him.

"Dallas?"

"It's Twister."

"Twister? When did we arrest him?"

"Earlier today. He tried to abduct Brody's Ker."

"What are you talking about?" Will pointed to the break room. "In here. I need my coffee and you look like you could use one too. Fill me in. And who is Ker?"

"That's right. You've been away on vacation. Brody's married. And her name is Ker." Dallas explained in a few succinct sentences what was going on. "Today, Twister appeared on the Foundation property and tried to get Ker to go with him. She outwitted him and ran for the building. Blair and Benen managed to trap him."

"And now he's dead? Is that what you're saying?"

"It is. Her mother is the one who hired him."

"Her mother? What was her last name?"

"Deeks. Her father ran a private investigations business. Ostensibly, it was run to go in and find missing and exploited children and teens. But we're finding out that there was a lot more to it than that. And now, her father is missing. We found his vehicle, burned, near where Brody and Ker were dumped."

"I see." Will rubbed at his head. "It doesn't pay to take a vacation. Too much happens when you're away."

Dallas laughed before he sobered. "That's true. I need to call Brody. I fear for them."

"I know what you mean, Dallas. Keep me up to speed, please."

—

"That I will. Oh, her father? He was friends with Bruce Carey."

"He was? Well, that certainly puts a wrinkle in it, doesn't it?"

Setting his phone done carefully, Brody rose from his desk chair, looking for Ker, finding her curled up on the couch, wrapped in a blanket, staring at the bandage on her hand.

"When does the bandage come off?" Brody dropped down beside her, an arm around her.

"In a couple of weeks. The surgeon thinks that it is healing well. Brody, who was that you were speaking with? Or shouldn't I ask?" She tucked her head up under his chin, finding comfort in that.

"Dallas. He had some bad news. Twister was killed tonight in the jail."

"He was? That's so sad. He never had a chance, did he?"

"No, I don't think he did. I mean, he made his choices in life, but it still doesn't mean that he had to die this way." Brody grew silent, content just to sit and hold his lady. "What are your thoughts about all this?"

"I'm just so confused, Brody. Everything that I have known all my life has been upturned. What if Dad is dead? Would Mom do that?"

"I don't know, Kitten. We don't know that your father is dead."

"I think that he is. Where they found his vehicle and where we were dumped? There are a lot of abandoned wells from old cottages. I'm surprised that they didn't drop us down into one."

"They could have, but I think that you'll find God intervened in that. I am still puzzled by that."

"I know. Did they take us as a threat towards Mom and Dad? Or did Mom arrange that as a threat against Dad?" Ker drew a deep breath. "Then, maybe something I overheard about a month ago and shrugged off makes sense."

"And that would be?"

"Dad and Mom were fighting, real angry words. He had accused her of stepping in on a case, making it impossible for him to reach the children that he needed to. They were gone when he got there. Mom had prevented him from leaving the day that he should have. What if Mom was playing both sides all along, and Dad found out?"

"That's a possibility. I can say that the fellows have thought of that, and are busily researching it."

"They are? No one said anything."

"No, they didn't, but from now on, we will. We just needed to make sure of our facts. After all, it is your family."

"A family that has held me back all my life." She sighed. "Brody, isn't tomorrow your potluck dinner?"

"It is. Why?"

"What do we take?"

"This time? It's our turn to bring a dessert. I have some squares in the freezer that I'll pull out unless you want to make something."

"No, it's okay. It's dressy, isn't it?"

"What do you mean?"

"I mean, dress clothes, and all that."

"Kitten, it's not. We are casual. Jeans, T-shirts. Some of the ladies wear those leggings that you seem so thrilled to find out that you like. Buckley quite often will appear in shorts and a polo shirt."

"Oh, I see." She shifted. "I would have dressed up in nice slacks, blouse, and heels. And been totally out of place."

"If you had dressed that way, then I would have been in dress slacks, dress shirt, tie, suit, whatever would make you comfortable."

"You would do that?"

"I would, Kitten. You are that important to me." He didn't say and wouldn't, not yet, that he was head over heels in love with her. He just prayed that she would respond when the time was right for him to tell her of his love.

Chapter 17

Three days later, Brody opened the door to the conference room, not surprised to find eleven other men there. Barnabas was involved in meetings, and Breck was out of town that day. He set down the mug of coffee that he was carrying, walking over to study the map.

"Do we have the location right?" Brendon approached him.

"You do. I don't get it. Why out there?"

"That's what we are working on."

"Ker said that there are a lot of abandoned wells out there." Brody paled. "How many? And is her father in one of them?" His voice was barely audible.

"Brody? Do you know what you just said?" Brendon looked around, finding the other men watching them.

"I do. I fear that is exactly where he is. How do we prove or disprove it?"

"I take Kade out. Do we have something that we can use to search from?" Bradon stood beside him, a hand on his shoulder.

"I'm not sure. Not likely. But we do need to search. With the search team?"

"Of course. I'll set it up."

"I won't say anything to Ker, not yet." Brody's body sagged for a moment, the sorrow he was anticipating dragging it down. "She is going through so much with her mother. She thinks that her mother had her father killed."

"That's what our feelings are." Bradon's hand tightened on his friend's shoulder. "We'll search, Brody. I'll talk to Dallas."

"Ker is scared. She's not saying much." Brody sighed. "This is wearing on her. To find out her mother has tried to have her abducted twice, charged in that, the man who tried to abduct her killed."

"We know, Brody." Buckley spoke from beside him, his eye on his friend. "Does she need to talk to someone?"

Brody shrugged. "She might. Right now, she's just trying to make sense of what happened." He shot a glance towards the door. "What I am about to say is more on the lines of a prayer request. She said her mother held her back all her life, told her what to wear, where to work. Chose her friends. She didn't realize how bad it was until now."

"And she's not sure what to do with all her freedom?" Blair shook his head. "And how does she feel about our ladies?"

Brody shared a look with him. "She is so glad to have them here. She feels overwhelmed at times, not sure how to approach them. Can I suggest that they just continue what they have been doing? Include her if that's what she wants."

"That they will do." Blair paused. "Devaney is quite concerned."

"I saw that." Brody paused, not wanting to break a confidence. "She's really not sure about her dress and what to wear when. If one of the ladies would help her out?"

"They will do that, and in a way that she would never know." Benen spoke from where he was standing beside Blair. "Cadee is quite taken with her."

"Ker has spoken about Cadee, wishing that she had had a friend like that years ago." Brody turned to face the room. "Now, where do we stand on the research?"

"About there." Burnie grinned at him. "We're finding all sorts of wonderful things about your in-laws. Her brother is still up north, I think?"

"I have no idea. Dallas has him stuck away somewhere, and isn't telling." Brody slid into the chair he usually used, reaching to boot up his computer. "What do we know about this Twister?"

"Nasty person, he was. Into a lot of stuff that would curl your hair." Baird sat beside Brody. "Here. This is for you and Ker. Read through it, talk it over, and then talk to one of us. It details a lot of what he was doing, and a lot of it was for her mother. Her father seems to have been on the edge of it all."

"So, if he found out and tried to stop her?" Brandon left his sentence unfinished.

"Would she remove him?" Brendon picked up the thought. "Somehow, I think that she would. I was

—

out to her hometown yesterday, Brody, and spoke with some of the merchants in town. Her mother is not liked. Her father was to some degree. Everyone knew what her mother was up to."

"How involved was the police force?"

"Some of them very much involved." Brendon slid another file folder towards him. "Ask her about these officers. See what her reaction is."

"You're throwing a lot at us." Brody glanced through the files, a grim look crossing his face.

"We are, Brody, just like we did for the others." Buckley looked up from where he was seated. "We need to dig deep on this one. I called Emma but she's away. Jace is working on something that has priority over everything else. He said they'd look at it as soon as they could."

Brody sighed. "That's all we can ask." He dropped his head onto his hand. "How do I keep her safe? She's finding her freedom and I can't fence her in, no matter the risk. And I can't be with her all the time."

"No, you can't. We'll pick up where we can. Our ladies will help. If she's out and about on the grounds, the security team has volunteered to trail her. There have also been calls from Dallas with names of officers if we need them."

"That's good." Brody answered absentmindedly, his thoughts already on the file he was reading.

—

Chapter 18

Throwing his truck into park a day later, Brody flung open his door and ran for the building. He hit the stairs still on a run, not waiting for the elevator. He fumbled with his keys, dropping them repeatedly before he was able to unlock the door and throw it open. Searching frantically for Ker, Brody stood in the hallway, not seeing her anywhere. *Where is she, Lord? Where is she? I got her text message and now she's not here.*

He paced back to the door, stepping into the hallway, finding Ker running down it, heading for him. He simply stood, his arms open, his stance widened as she hit him full force, tears streaming down her face. His face on her hair, Brody watched as Cadee and Ennis approached, worry on their faces.

"What happened, Ker?"

"Mom was here. I could hear her at the door. How did she get in?" Ker leaned back, staring up at him. "Cadee and Ennis were here. Cadee checked to make sure the way was clear and took me to their apartment, to wait for you. What did she want?"

"I don't, my love, but she's not to be here. Ladies, did you see her?"

"We did. We peeked out after Ker did. She was smart, Brody. She didn't answer the door and kept really quiet as she looked out." Ennis rubbed at Ker's back. "Now, what do we do? How do we keep you safe?"

"That's what I would like to know." Ker hugged Brody tighter. "I can't do much more of this, Brody. This is how she is. She keeps hitting at you until you give in."

"But you see, you have secret weapons. You have all of us here, the police force, friends who will step in." He looked up at the ladies waiting. "Ladies, how be you find all the rest of you and come back? We need to make some plans. The fellows have been working on something, but you ladies need to be in on this."

"How be we meet in the conference room? An unscheduled potluck dinner sounds good to me." Ennis grinned. "And no, Ker, you don't have to bring anything, except yourself. And Brody, if you want to." She waved as she walked away, Cadee beside her, Brody's laughter following them.

"Did she really do that? Plan a meal without asking anyone else?" Ker was dumbfounded, staring after her friends.

"She did. It's what we do. It's not the first time that we have met like this, researching and planning, with the ladies planning a meal for us. Come on. I need to change and you need to find that cup of tea that I know you didn't finish."

Ker sighed. "No, I didn't finish it." She made no move from his arms, and he made no move to release her.

—

He finally turned them to the apartment. "As much as I enjoy having you in my arms, we do need to meet with the others."

Ker just looked at him, not quite sure what he meant before she headed for her neglected cup of tea, not caring that it was cold, her thoughts on Brody, and just what he had meant. She knew in her heart that he was the knight that she had dreamed about, that she was falling in love with him. Her hand paused as it set her cup down. Did he really call me his love? Lord, did I hear right? If I did, then we need to talk, don't we? Protect him, dear Lord. Let no harm come to him.

Watching the men closely as she helped to clear up from the meal, Ker frowned. They were joking and teasing one another, even as they bent over files or stared at computer screens. She could see Barnabas and Brady at the map, pointing at different areas.

Imly had been watching her. "Not used to this?"

Ker shook her head. "It seems like chaos, to tell you the truth."

"Organized chaos. They do this, teasing one another, just to relieve the stress. Soon, they'll be bouncing ideas and thoughts off one another. They work well together. God brought them together, years ago, and it has been a blessing to all of us."

"That He did, Ker." Devaney took the tray out of Ker's hands. "Each of the men, with the exception of Breck and Barnabas, are from each of the other provinces and territories. Those two are from Ontario, this area, and have been friends for life. Barnabas searched for these fellows, watching them, finding out about them, before he offered them employment and a home. God had to be the one making the decision, he said. It was God who has led them here."

"They all have unique talents. Not just in their work. They also volunteer." Berneen snapped the lid back on a casserole dish. "Your Brody? Did he tell you that he tutors preteens in English? No? He does. He doesn't like a lot of praise, but we hear talk from them. The parents are blessed with his compassion for the young ones."

"He did hint at that." Ker leaned back against the table. "But what do I do? I can't go back to where I was. Not that I want to."

"Take your time to make a decision. Talk to Brody. Talk to anyone of us. Talk to Breck or Barnabas. As for now, enjoy the time that you are not working." Fynn pointed to her hand. "That still needs to heal, doesn't it?"

"It does." Ker sighed. "I just wish things were different."

"We all have had that wish, Ker." Hagen spoke up. "All of us."

—

Chapter 19

Brody stared at the man blocking his path before he moved backward. He didn't know him, but he didn't think the man was there for the good of Brody's health. Coming to an abrupt halt as he felt something poke him in his back, his hands raised.

"I think you have the wrong person. I don't have anything that you would want."

"On the contrary, Mr. Corcoran, you do. We need you to have Ker come here. And now." The man facing him approached to stand with two feet of him.

"No, not happening. I won't bring her here." Driven to his knees by the vicious blow to his back, Brody drew in as deep a breath as he could. "Was that really necessary?"

"Absolutely. You need to cooperate with us, Mr. Corcoran. Bring Ker here." The man repeated his request, studying his fingernails on his right hand as he did so.

"I told you. That's not happening."

Five minutes later, the second man stepped away from Brody, staring down at the bloodied body in front of him, tucking away the brass knuckles that he had used on Brody.

"That didn't work. He just wouldn't cooperate with us."

"No, he wouldn't." The first man looked around before he turned away. "I told her that it wouldn't."

"Ker is too well protected." The second man stared back at Brody. "You know, is the pay really worth it?"

"I know what you mean." The first man turned, before he searched for a payphone, making an anonymous call about a man down. "Let's hit the road. I hear the weather out west is better for our health."

"She'll track us down." The man slipped into the seat of the car.

"Not if we're careful. I have a stash of aliases that we can use. Let's pack what we need and blow this town."

Brady drew in a deep breath as he approached Brody, his eyes finding those of his partner, Patrick.

"Brody? What on earth? Brady?" Patrick was on his knees beside Brody, Brady on the other side.

"Whoever did this worked him over well." Brady studied him. "And not with his fists."

Dallas had heard the call and headed their way. He studied his friend. "Brass knuckles."

"Brass knuckles? They still use them?" Patrick's comment was low, even as he and Brady worked to stabilize Brody. "Where all is he hurt?"

"A better question would be where isn't he." Brady rolled Brody to one side, a deep groan coming from his friend. "His back is really bruised." He slipped the shirt back down. "Okay, when you're ready, let's move him and get him in. Dallas? Ker?"

"I'll call Breck. Have him bring her in." Dallas paused. "They'll need an escort."

"Have the patrol vehicle meet them on the way in. I won't want to answer to Ker if she's delayed waiting for that."

Dallas stared at him. "Just what does that mean?"

"You didn't hear? Apparently, she was ticked off at Brody when Brandon and Benen found them. She threw her shoes at him. So, I wouldn't want to be the one not telling her right away." The men moved away, their equipment boxes gathered up, Brady's eye on Brody, watching him closely.

Answering her door, Ker stared at Breck and then Ennis.

"Come in, you two. What can I do for you?"

Breck stepped inside, his frown deepening. "We need you to come with us, Ker. Brody has been hurt. Dallas is sending a patrol car to meet us."

"Brody? I just spoke with him, about twenty minutes ago. How could that be?" Ker refused to move.

"Ker, we need you to move and move now. Brody is on his way to the hospital. Brady is with him. Dallas would not be sending out a car unless he felt it was urgent and necessary."

Ker's face paled. "She got to him! I hate her!" She turned and ran for a jacket, and her purse, struggling to pull on sneakers as she returned. "Well? What are we standing here for? Are you driving?" She pulled the door closed, locking it, and then running for the stairs.

Breck stared after her, shooting a look at Ennis. "Is she for real?"

"Oh, yeah! Hurry, Breck. She just might jimmy open the doors on your truck, hotwire it, and take off." Ennis ran after Ker, finding her waiting just inside the lobby door.

"Well? Is he coming or are you driving?"

Ennis broke out into laughter. "Ker, even in your fright, you are just too funny for words. Here he is. Quick. I told him that you'd jimmy the lock and hotwire his truck."

"You did what?" Ker stared at her before shooting a look at Breck. "You know, I just might do that."

Ker was out of the truck and running for the door to the hospital before Breck could even come to a full stop, Ennis behind her. He shook his head, found a parking spot, and ran after them. Dallas met him just inside the door, pointing to the examination rooms.

"She's back there already. Doc was watching for her."

"He was? Good. Any word?"

"Not a lot. He's been beaten badly, Breck. And not with just fists."

"No?" Breck's eyes slid closed. "Don't tell me."

—

"I won't, then. We both know what was used. Doc's not saying much, nor did Brady. I'll keep an officer with him for now."

"Ker won't leave him. I can guarantee you that. If we try, she'll hide somewhere and sneak back to be with him."

"That's our assessment. We'll clear it." Dallas watched as Ennis returned, walking towards them. "Ennis?"

"She's with him. She made me leave." Ennis brushed a tear away. "He looks awful, Breck."

"I'm sure he does. Here, have a seat. I'll send out a text and let them know what's going on. Dallas?"

"I've been called to another case. I'll touch base when I can. Have Ker call me with any news." Dallas walked away, his heart sore for his friend and his wife. Why, Lord? I just don't get it. Not anymore. I just don't understand the evil that's out there today, and touching so many of my friends.

Chapter 20

Her hand resting on Brody's cheek, feeling the stubble on it, the cuts and scrapes from his beating, Ker blinked back tears. I don't get it, Lord. Why? She bent to drop a kiss on his cheek, before she raised back up, to stand watching him.

Doc stood watching her in turn before he nodded. Anna was right, once more. She had insisted that the young couple were in love, just not ready to let each other know. This may do it, Anna. And Lord, he's going to need a real touch of the hem of the Master's garment. I haven't seen someone beaten like this in a while.

Doc's arm around her shoulders startled Ker for a moment before she relaxed against him. Doc had become like a father to her, and she needed that father right now.

"Doc?" Her voice was a mere whisper.

"He's hurt bad, Ker. Has anyone talked to you? No? Then, I guess I must. Dallas has confirmed from what he's seen that brass knuckles were used. We can see the marks that they left. That being said, we need to talk about his injuries."

"Is he going to die, Doc? I can't handle it if he does. I won't want to live if he does." Ker didn't take her gaze from Brody.

"No, but he will need time to heal. For starters, he has massive bruising all over. His kidneys are bruised, and we need to watch them. His liver has a laceration. But it's his spleen. He's bleeding from it."

"And you need to go in and remove it?"

"That's what the surgeon is deciding now. We will make no decision without talking with you first. Is someone with you?"

Ker nodded. "Ennis was with Breck. She's in the waiting room." Her voice died away. Doc could barely hear her next comment. "And this is when I could really use my Mom. Only Mom is the one who did this."

Doc hugged her to him. "Let me call Anna for you."

Ker nodded. "Thank you."

Anna approached her, much as Doc had, not saying anything, just gathering her close, holding her as she would her own daughter. She felt the shudders and then the sobs as Ker broke down. Breck's hand on Anna's back directed the ladies to a chair. He watched, compassion on his face before he looked up. Anger took over for a moment, before he turned, finding the men of the building standing around him.

"Who?" Brendon spoke for the group.

"Her mother, we think. The man or men who did this were long gone." Breck frowned. "It was strange. There was an anonymous call that came in from a payphone."

"Guilty conscience?" Buckley held up hope.

"Possibly. Right now, Brody is headed for surgery. Ker needs us. Where do we stand with the investigation?"

"Not where we need to be. That's a given." Brandon paced, a prayer raising for his friend.

"What do we do now, then? Seek until we find the answers?" Burnie spoke up. "It's like trying to solve one of those puzzles that have only one solution and we don't know how to find it."

Brennen stared at him. "Burnie, how do you do it? You just said the magic words."

"I did? And what would that be?"

"A puzzle. Like in a logic problem. What we need to do is draw up one of those diagrams and work it like you would one of those problems." Brennen's eyes had lit up.

"I see what you mean. Of course, it's a puzzle. They all are." Burnie paced before he drew out a pad of paper and clicked his pen to open it. "Okay, so we brainstorm. We'll have some time. We split up in teams like we usually do."

The men worked away, quiet conversation among them, glancing up every once in a while to check on Ker. Buckley sat for the longest time, his eyes closed, his heart hurting for his friends. *Why, Lord? I don't get it. Not at all. How do we trust? How do we seek to find the answers? I know You care, that You will heal. It's just so hard to see this young lady hurting and hurting because of her family.*

Ker sat, her eyes on the door to the operating room that she could barely see around the corner, her cheeks wet with her tears. Anna's arm was around her, her hand in Ennis' as they sat with her, whispered prayers murmured every once in a while. The other ladies had been in and out, checking on her, whispering a prayer or a Bible verse. She had simply nodded, her eyes not moving.

How long, Lord, just how long do I have to wait? It's not fair and it's not right. I hate my mother for this, and that I know I shouldn't do. How do I forgive when she has caused so much hate and destruction? The men don't have to say. I can read it on their faces. She sank back, her hand reaching for the bottle of water Fynn was handing her, to simply twist it in her hands.

Doc watched for a while before he returned to his duties. He never understood how families could hurt one another like this. He saw it all too frequently in the Emergency Department. He had had a quick word with the surgeon, whose grim look had not boded well for Brody.

Hours later, Ker was on her feet, moving rapidly towards the surgeon as he appeared, pulling the surgical cap from his head, his mask tucked down under his chin.

"Doctor? How is he?"

"He's in recovery, Ker. May I call you that?" At her nod, he continued. "We had to resect the spleen. That is, we had to remove it. He can live without it, just needs to take precautions, that's all. The liver laceration was not as bad as we feared. It will heal on

---

its own. The kidneys are bruised. Those we need to watch. Overall, considering the beating that he took, I was surprised not to find more internal bleeding."

"I'm not. God had His hand on him."

"If you say so. Now, he's in recovery right now. Once we can stabilize him more, we'll move him to a room. Likely ICU for the night. And yes, you can see him once we get him moved." He looked around the room, surprised to find himself the centre of attention from so many eyes. "These people are with you?"

"They are. For all intents and purposes, they are my family and Brody's. Just don't take too long to get me to him." Ker moved away, back towards Anna who had stood, ready to hug Ker to her again.

"Ker?"

"He's in recovery. Lost his spleen. Needs to be careful. He's going to ICU soon." She looked around at the room, not surprised at the silence. "Thank you. Thank you for being here. Thank you for the support. Thank you for praying." Her legs gave way, Brennen there to catch her and help her to a chair. "I don't know why I did that."

"Release of stress. It happens, Ker." Brennen crouched in front of her, taking the bottle of juice handed him to give to her. "Here. Drink this. And drink all of it. You need it."

"Yes, boss." Ker drank deeply, her eyes closed, not seeing the grins on the faces of the men. They were beginning to understand how she thought.

Chapter 21

Searching for Ker the next afternoon, Dallas finally found her in the waiting room of the surgical floor, standing in front of a window. Her stature was hunched, and he could see the hurt in it. He sighed. Why, Lord, again he questioned. What do they want from her?

"Ker?" Dallas gently touched her shoulder. "Is Brody worse?"

Ker shook her head, her hair moving with the motion. She pulled at a lock. "I used to wear my hair in a braid or a ponytail all the time. Mom made me. It became just too hard to fight her on it. I don't know. Brody likes it down." She looked up at him, a lost little girl look in her eyes. "Why is she like this, Dallas? Have you found out yet?"

"Not yet. Here, Ker. Sit. First, tell me about Brody."

Folding her arms around herself, Ker shuddered. "He's back in surgery, Dallas. They did some sort of imaging this morning and found something or other bleeding. The surgeon didn't think that they could wait."

"Oh, Ker! And you've been here on your own?" At her nod, he shook his head. "Let me call one of the ladies for you." He looked up. "Wait. Here are Ennis and Devaney. They will sit with you."

"Thank you. I didn't want to bother anyone." Her voice was almost too low to hear.

"It is never a bother, Ker. We are family." Ennis hugged her and sat beside her. "Now, Dallas is here. Did he say why?"

Ker stared at her and then at Dallas. "No, he hasn't. I don't think he's here for his own health."

Dallas stared at her before he shook a finger at her, a grin briefly appearing on his face. "Behave, Mrs. Corcoran."

Ker blushed and then spoke, a wistful tone to her voice. "I think you are one of the first to address me as that. It's like it never happened." Her voice faltered. "Do you know where Keefe is?"

"I do. And you want to talk to him? I can see what I can arrange about that. He's one I needed to talk to you about today."

"How deep is he into all this?"

"Not at all. Just like you. He didn't know anything. He knew about the threats and packages but not what your mother was up to. He told me that your father insisted that he take the two weeks off that he did."

"Dad did? And he called in Brody on a pretence. I understand that now. He was protecting us. How much does he know?"

"That we will ask him when we find him."

"And just how sure are you that he is alive?"

Dallas pulled out his phone and sorted through his photos, pausing at one. "I am going to show you a photo, Ker. I need you to tell me if you recognize it."

Ker took his phone, her eyes searching his for a moment before she looked down. Her fingers covered her trembling lips even as she blinked back tears. "Dad! What did she do?"

"You confirm that this is your father?" Ker nodded at his question. "He was found about one hundred miles from here, unconscious and with no identification on him. I have been in touch with a detective there. Your father is still unconscious, but we have now placed him under police guard."

Ker's face hardened. "She just doesn't stop. Do we even know why?"

"We are working on that, Ker. Trying our best to solve it. The fellows are working on a thought that one of them had. It may take some time, but we will get there."

"I know. I just don't know how much time we'll have. That's the thing." Ker was on her feet, moving towards the surgeon as he approached.

"Ker? These are friends of yours?" He nodded towards the group.

"They are. That's the police detective." Ker looked back at them. "You can talk in front of them if you like."

"I would. I also need to sit for a few moments. I have been here doing surgeries since midnight."

"You have? That's not good." Ker sat, waiting for him to speak, Ennis and Devaney reaching for her hands.

"How are you holding up, Ker, first of all?"

She shrugged. "I have no idea. I'm here where I need to be. And I am scared. Scared for Brody. Scared that my mother or one of her henchmen will appear."

"And that is an issue?"

"It is. She's the one responsible for this. For putting Brody in there. For making my father and brother disappear from my life. What else would you like to know?"

The surgeon, Dr. Wight, just shook his head. "We'll take precautions for you and Brody, Ker. Now about Brody. We went in, as we told you we had to, to find the bleeding. It was from the liver laceration. We've done what we need to for now. We'll wait for a day or so, and redo the imaging for him."

"And if he's still bleeding?"

"That we will address as we need to. For now, he is stable. We'll monitor him. Give us about an hour, and then the nurse will come for you. He's in recovery right now."

"Thank you, Dr. Wight. You are a blessing from God." Ker's words startled the surgeon as he stood, and he studied her for a moment before he turned and walked away with a thoughtful look on his face.

Chapter 22

Finally back beside Brody, Ker watched as he moved restlessly before she reached to lay a hand on his shoulder. His movements stopped for a moment before his head began to toss and turn.

She bent closer to try and understand what he was muttering, her face paling as she did so. He had been beaten because he refused to bring her to the men? Anger once more surged through her and then faded. Lord? I am trying to forgive, but it's hard. I need to seek for Your peace but it's just not so easy. I need to hear Brody's prayers for me, for us. And I can't. Lord, please? Heal my husband.

She bent close again, to lay her cheek against his, finding that gesture stilled him. She stayed like that even as she continued to pray before she dropped a kiss on his cheek and whispered that she needed him. He had all of her love, and she wanted to grow old with him.

An hour later, Brody's eyes flickered as he fought his way out of the darkness towards the light flickering between his eyelids. He finally managed to open them, his gaze wandering across the ceiling and then around the room. Disoriented, he tried to raise himself but his pain kept him flat on the bed. A groan came from him, and he looked around to see who had groaned.

Ker was on her feet, her hand reaching for his, her eyes watchful, even as Brody's gaze found hers.

"Hi! Do I know you?" Brody's voice was hoarse.

Ker just shook her head. "You should. We married."

"Married? No, I don't think so. I'm tired. And why am I in a hospital room?" Brody's head moved restlessly until Ker placed her hand back against his cheek.

"Because you were beaten severely. You've had surgery, Brody. And you can't be moving around."

"I will if I want to." Brody pulled himself upright despite her protests, an arm clamped around his abdomen before he fell back. "I hurt."

"Yes, you do. You have had major surgery, twice in the last day. So, stay still." Ker was getting angry with him and then relaxed. It wasn't his fault, now was it?

Brody's eyes closed as he drifted off, his hand reaching for hers, his grip tight. She just shook her head and then looked behind her. There was no way that she could reach her chair, and he was just not letting go of her.

Breck studied the couple for a moment from where he stood in the doorway, shaking his head finally as he walked towards them. He reached to pull Ker's chair closer, earning himself a soft thank you.

"He's been awake?"

"He has." Breck grinned at the disgruntled tone. "He says that we're not married. And then he wanted to get up."

Breck's head tilted as he studied their linked hands. "He may have said that. I know that he doesn't handle coming around from anesthesia too well. But that grip on your hand? That tells me that he doesn't want you to move away from him. He may not say it in words, Ker, but he is deeply in love with you."

"He is? I need to hear it. Actions don't prove anything, not lately." Ker was disheartened but also cheered by Breck's words.

Brody had awakened once more, listening to the voices, Ker's voice calming him even with the frustration he could hear in it. Breck was right, he thought. I don't do anesthesia well.

Breck caught a slight movement on Brody's part and his attention shifted to him.

"Brody? You awake?"

"I am. What do you want?"

"Nothing much. Just wanted to see how you were faring. I hear tell you are giving the love of your life a hard time." Breck just grinned at the frown Ker sent his way.

"I am? I wouldn't do that." Brody's eyes opened again, and he squinted in the light. "Where am I again?"

"In the hospital, my friend. Someone beat you up pretty badly."

"Is that why I hurt? I don't remember much." Brody suddenly jerked upright. "They wanted me to bring Ker to them. I couldn't do that. I need to find her."

"She's right here, my friend. You're holding pretty tight to her hand." Breck laughed at the expression on Brody's face. "It's okay, Brody. Lay back down. We don't want you to undo all the stitches that the surgeon decided you needed."

"Stitches? I don't do stitches. I thought I told you that."

"You might have but they didn't have much choice. Ker, make him lie still, will you? I have a meeting to get to but I'll be back. I'll let the others know that Brody is awake and running true to form." Breck's laughter sounded behind as he left.

Ker stared after him, knowing he wasn't laughing at them or making fun of them before she felt a tug on her hand. She turned back, to find Brody watching her intently.

"Ker? Are you okay?"

"I am now. An hour ago, you told me that you weren't married."

"I did? I certainly didn't mean that. You are the one I love, Ker. No other. I'm sorry if I made you sad." Brody watched as she frowned at him.

"Not sad, Brody. Mad. Mad at my mother for all this."

"I know, Kitten. I know." He tugged at her hand even as he reached to raise the head of the bed. "No, don't stop me. I need to sit up." He wrapped her in his arm, his head on hers. "What all have you been told?"

"About you? That you no longer have a spleen, that the liver laceration had to be dealt with again this morning, that your kidneys are bruised. Not to say anything about all the other bruises and cuts."

"I'll get better. But have you heard anything else?"

"Dallas was around. He has talked to Keefe, who knows nothing of what was going on. Keefe told Dallas that Dad made him take those two weeks of vacation. And then he called you in. He was trying to protect us, wasn't he?"

"I think he was. He must have found out something and knew you two were in danger."

"And Dallas has found Dad. He was found unconscious somewhere with no identification on him. Dallas had me identify him from a picture." Her head went against Brody even as she struggled with her tears. "Why, Brody? I just don't get it."

"I don't either. The fellows are working on something, that much I know. How long am I in here for?"

"Dr. Wight didn't say. I wish this was over, Brody."

"I do too. I have a beautiful lady right here beside me that I want to live life with and right now we can't."

____

"We can, Brody. We can." Ker turned to him. "I refuse to let her win, to dictate how I live my life anymore. Breck questioned me this morning about my hair, for some reason. I realized then that what I was doing was following Mom's rules for me. It's not how I want to live. I don't like dressing up and being on stage all the time. That's how she made me feel."

Brody hugged her tighter to him, not letting her see his grimace of pain. "Then, we take back your life and make it our life. We start today, my love."

Chapter 23

Her arms wrapped around herself, Ker stood in their kitchen doorway two days later, her eyes on Brody. She could hear the quiet conversation behind her from Cadee and Guenivere, as they moved about, preparing a meal, putting away what they didn't need that had been delivered by the building family. She sighed. Brody was being typical, she thought, not wanting help but needing it.

"I don't want to lie down." Brody was protesting, his finger pointing to the living room. Brandon and Buckley exchanged glances and shook their heads.

"You need to rest, Brody. That's what the surgeon said. As in bed. Lying down." Brandon tried to steer his friend that way as both he and Buckley held him upright by their grasps on his arms.

"Absolutely not." Brody finally shrugged off their hands, wrapping an arm around himself, and shuffling to the living room, to drop down on the couch, his eyes closing from pain and fatigue. "I'm sorry, fellows. I know that you're trying to help. But I don't want to go in there. Not yet."

"Brody? You do realize that you just had major surgery, don't you?" Brandon sat down near him.

"How can I forget? Everyone keeps reminding me." Brody squinted through one open eye at his friend. "Now, tell me. Where do we stand with what we are looking at?"

"Not today, Brody. Tomorrow." Ker finally moved in, simply picking up his feet and making him lie back on the pillows that she had already positioned on the couch. "Today, it is enough that you are at home. Tomorrow, someone will come up here, bring what they can for you to look at and we'll talk. Today, you'll do what I say."

"And if I don't?" Brody knew he was petulant but felt he deserved to be. He hurt all over, more than he had in the hospital.

"Remember, I have a good pitching arm. And I have shoes handy." Ker perched beside him. "Please, Brody? I don't want to have to wake anyone up in the middle of the night to take you back in. And if you keep up this way, I will." She rose and walked away from him, heading for the kitchen.

Brandon looked after her before he exchanged a glance with Buckley, who simply nodded at Brody. Brody had sank back onto the pillows, his eyes closed in his white face, pain drawn on it.

"She's right. I just want this over yesterday." Brody's voice was gruff.

"We know you do, Brody. But you do have to take care. Ker wants you around for a long time. So do the rest of us." Brandon was on his feet. "I need to run. I have my volunteer work later. Call if you need anything."

"Thanks again, Brandon."

"No problem. You were there for us when we went through what we did. It's our turn to return the favour."

Buckley studied his friend. "How can I pray for you best, Brody?"

"Pray this over and quickly. For her father and brother. For resolution of whatever it is that needs to be resolved. For Ker. This is hitting her hard. She won't show it unless it comes out in anger. Right now, she's dealing with that and trying to find out how to forgive her mother."

"We have been doing just that, Brody. But for you two, how do I pray on a personal level?"

Brody shrugged, his eyes closing. "I don't know, Buckley. I really don't know." He lost the battle to stay away and slept.

Ker stood watching. "He's asleep."

"He is, Ker. And will do this off and on for a few days, I suspect. Now, what I asked him? How do I pray for you?"

Ker shrugged. "What he said. I really have never had anyone ask me that before, do you know?"

"I gathered that. I'm off. I see the ladies are gone. Call one of us, no matter the time of day or night, do you understand?"

Ker reached to hug him, surprising herself. "Thank you, Buckley. You are what I imagined a minister should be like." She stood, listening as Buckley walked away, the door closing quietly behind him before she sank to a sitting position beside the couch, her arm across Brody, her hand on his cheek. Tears sparkled on her cheeks as she prayed, asking for forgiveness and strength. She knew they were not done yet, not by a long mile, as her father would have put it.

Chapter 24

Brody stirred, his hand reaching for his phone, hearing it ringing. He couldn't find it, but his hand stopped as he saw Ker sitting just as she had sat a few hours previously. Worn out, she too slept. He smiled, before he reached for his phone, frowning at the text message. This is not good, he thought. Her mother's in the area. She's been spotted but how do we stop her? She'll harm Ker unless we do.

Carefully sitting up, he reached down, not listening to his body, to scoop Ker close to him and up onto the couch. She turned into him, and he dropped a kiss on her hair. Lord, it's coming up to that point where it gets so dangerous. With her mother here, looking for her, we both have to be so careful. Who knows what she will do to either one of us. I fear for her.

He rose, walking slowly through the apartment, before he stood, staring at his face in the bathroom mirror. He winced, seeing the varied colours of the bruising and the cuts and lacerations. I am thankful, Lord, that I survived. They wanted Ker, but something seemed off. Why there, Lord? He shrugged, turning on the water in the shower, knowing it would hurt but he needed to clean up and shave. He hated the smell of the hospital that always lingered.

Ker stood and waited for Brody to return, not sure what he would want. She had received a text message from her mother, and the viciousness of it frightened her as no other message ever had. Lord, she whispered, I thought that she was a believer. She worked in the church. She has hidden this from us all. I need a mother, and I don't have one. She wiped at the tears, jumping as she felt arms around her.

"Kitten?"

She would never have thought of that word as a term of endearment but Brody had made it theirs.

"Mom sent a text message. She is getting more brutal. What did I do to make her like that?"

"It was that bad?" He took the phone she thrust at him. "Ker? You really are in danger. We can't let you out anywhere." He forwarded the message to his own phone and then on to Dallas. "She's here in the area, isn't she?"

"She has to be. I just don't understand what she wants. I'm not in her life. Keefe is in hiding. She's made Dad disappear. I don't think that she planned for him to be found."

"Not likely. But she has lost control of all three of you." Brody moved away, reaching for the mug of coffee that she had poured for him, sitting at the table. "Let's have something to eat, and then make some plans."

"I don't know what plans that we can make. We have no idea what she's planning." Ker slid bowls of soup onto the table for them. "I'm sorry. I didn't cook this. In fact, I'm not that great a cook. I was never allowed to cook."

Brody reached for her hand, blessing their food, and then speaking softly. "We'll learn together. I had to, Ker, just to survive. Anna was a great teacher. She'll work with you."

"But she'll judge me. I just know that." Ker's voice held defeat.

"Not at all. Anna loves to teach cooking and baking. She's always finding something new to do just that. She misses having her daughter around all the time. The ladies in the building are precious to her."

Ker shrugged. "What did we need to talk about?"

"First, before I was hurt, the fellows were making progress in what they think your mother was involved in. It's not pretty."

"Did you think it would be? Given what Dad did, finding missing and exploited children and teens, was Mom involved on the other side?"

"That's what we've heard. We are still working to confirm that. Dallas has been given what we have and he has someone working on it as well." Brody paused, his spoon halfway to his mouth before he lowered it. "Is there a particular point in time where your mother seemed to change?"

Ker stared at him. "You know, I think there was. Let me think for a moment." She ate absentmindedly. "About the time I turned fifteen and Keefe sixteen. She had always been hard, but she became harder on us, harsher. We could do nothing right. I think that over time, beaten down as she had us, we just gave up and let her control us."

———

"What was your Dad working on at the time? Was he always involved in this type of rescue?"

Ker stared at him, surprise on her face. "No, he wasn't. He used to do other stuff, I'm not sure what now. But about that time, I can remember him being approached by a friend's father. Their young son had gone missing, and he wanted Dad to find him. The boy was around seven, I think. Dad found him, and that decided him to change his investigations to that."

"So, if your Mom was involved in these disappearances, she wouldn't want your father involved in tracking the children and teens." Brody rose, paused to catch his balance, and then moved to clear the table with Ker's help. "Now, Ker, we have something to work with. Let's head for the office."

"Not tonight, Brody. Tonight, you rest. You need that." She stood in the hallway, refusing to let him pass. "The only way past me is if you head for the bedroom. Other than that, it's the living room and the couch. Please?"

Brody just swept her into a hug, and turned them to the living room, sinking down gratefully.

"Thank you, Kitten. I really didn't want to go there, but I want this over for you."

"And we'll get there. I just hate that she has done this to you."

"I hate how she's treated you, beaten you down. I know you're angry. I would be too if I were you. But don't let the anger consume you."

"I'm trying, Brody. I'm trying, but it's hard. Buckley asked me how he could pray for me. That's all I could think of."

"And he will have already been praying that way. He's good at reading people." Brody grew silent, content, he thought, just to sit there, holding the love of his life. "We still need to talk, Kitten."

She twisted to look up at him, reading him correctly. "And we will. Right now, hush. You're talking too much." She smirked as he grinned at her and then kissed her forehead.

Chapter 25

The next morning, Brody sat at the table in the conference room, eyeing the boards on the wall, amazed at how much work that his friends had done. He shook his head at Ker as she hovered near him.

"Sit, Kitten. We'll find out what's going on." He groaned as his phone chimed. He stared at the text before he handed her the phone.

"Brody? What is it?" Ker stared down at the text. "This can't be right. Mom wouldn't do that. At least, I don't think that she would."

"Brody? You look troubled." Barnabas sat beside him.

"Here. Ker's mother has gone to the media, stating that Ker is being held against her will by us."

"I heard that this morning. Our lawyers are already dealing with it. They want a statement from you two, to pass on." Barnabas paused. "I don't know where your relationship is right now. That's none of my business. But in the video, we need you to look happy and together."

"That's not a problem." Ker looked up at him, anger making her eyes spark. "I know how she thinks. We'll make her eat her words, in more ways than one. What can we do in the meantime to help move this along?"

Barnabas stared at her for a moment. "Tell us whatever you can about your mother, what she was involved with. What you can without breaking confidentiality on your father's cases. What was your brother involved with? That will help."

"How long a day do you have? I could talk for hours. I'm finally ready to." She looked at Brody, finding him watching her, his trust in her evident. "Brody and I figured out last night about when she changed. I was fifteen, Keefe sixteen." She detailed the account for him, not realizing that there was silence in the room, and that her voice carried to everyone.

"Do you think she was involved in that?" Brendon had moved closer, taking notes.

"I do. Her reaction was off if I remember. She wasn't that concerned, not like she should have been. Dad was. It drove him night and day to find them." She looked up at Brandon. "They found the boy, hurt but alive. They never found who kidnapped him. And he never said. Whether it was because he didn't know or because he was too scared, that didn't become clear at all."

"Can you let us have the names? I'll pass them on to Dallas." Brandon took the paper that she handed him. "Prepared, were you?"

Ker shrugged. "It's just habit, I guess. I used to make notes of everything and anything." Her face grew sad. "With my house gone, all of that is gone."

"I'm sorry, Ker. That should not have happened. Brennen, did we get the report on that?" Barnabas looked around.

"We did. Emma found it for us. She's back, Brody, and working on this." Brennen handed over the file folder. "It was arson. I'm sorry, Ker, that it happened."

Ker nodded. "It is what it is, isn't it? We can't go back. Things can be replaced." She looked up at Brody. "And to tell you the truth, now that I no longer have the house, I'm glad. Mom picked it out, decorated it, and all. I had no say in anything. If I did say something, she just ignored me and went her own way."

Barnabas made a sound, his eyes meeting Brody. "This is Brody's place to say it, Ker, but understand. If there is something in the apartment that you want changed in any way, at any time, talk to us. It will happen. It is your home as well as Brody's. The ladies have made changes to their own places, just to make it theirs. Yours is no different." Barnabas was on his feet, walking out of the room before Ker could respond.

She stared after him, then reached for the folder, opening it and reading through the report. She frowned when she finished, going back to something that had puzzled her.

"I don't understand this. It says the fire started in the gas stove, that it had been tampered with. I didn't have a gas stove. That was one thing that I refused. Mom could not change my mind on that."

"You didn't? That's interesting. We never thought to ask you. What about the dryer?"

"Electric. So was the water heater. If it says different, then someone has changed them. And it had to be that day. What did she do?"

"We'll find out. Now that we know, we can start canvassing the companies."

"Wait. She has a friend who is a gas fitter. She would have had him do it. He would have gotten the appliances as well." Ker reached for another piece of paper. "This is who he is. He's not that well liked in the community."

"Thank you, Ker. We'll handle this." Bradon reached for it. "Now, Brody looks as if he's going to faint or something."

"I know. Would someone help us, please?" She stood, a hand on Brody's shoulder. "But before we leave, may I thank each one of you? I know you're not doing it for thanks, but you have no idea what this means to me."

Brody rose with Brady's assistance, and then headed out, his arm around his bride, Brady's hand under his other arm.

"Brody? What are your thoughts?"

"My thoughts? Someone is setting it up to make Ker look like she is unstable. I don't like that. This is just an opening wedge, I suspect. Let Barnabas know we want to do that video for him. And today. I want the world to see what her mother has done."

"But you know that people will say it was Ker who arranged it."

"I know. Ker, your phone please." He took it when she offered it to him, a puzzled look on her face. "Hand this off to Dallas, please. Have the techs go over it. Ker has had no access to any phone other than mine, and I know that it hasn't been used for that. She hasn't been in town to use any payphones, either."

"I'll need yours too, Brody. I'll grab a phone from the security team for now for you two."

Chapter 26

Ker's mother stared at the television, anger growing within in, disfiguring her face. She threw the glass she was holding, just missing the screen, having it shatter against the wall, liquid running down to the floor. How dare she, she thought? How dare she go on television and into the papers with that story? Who would believe her, anyway?

She paced the room, Ker's voice detailing her life and what had transpired in the last few weeks. Brody was beside her, an arm around her, her hand tight in his. His face looked garish in the lighting, the varied colours showing clearly what had happened.

One of the Foundation lawyers drew them out, asking the questions that would tell the story. Her mother sneered. A likely story, she thought. Of course, Ker had gas appliances. She had seen to that. It just didn't matter that Ker hadn't known that they had been replaced. Her car had been in the driveway. She was supposed to have been home that day and died in the fire. Why hadn't she? Who had mixed that up?

Ker looked directly at the camera as she finished, Brody's arm tightening around her. They had talked about what they needed to say. Ker had been adamant that she would address her mother.

"Mom, I know that you are out there and listening. You always listen to the news. Well, this time, you're the news. I want it out there that you tried to kill me. You tried to kill my beloved Brody. I have no idea what you tried with Keefe. Or what you did to Dad. But this ends now. If you come after me again, you will not win. I refuse to let you control me anymore. I don't know what made you change, or if you were always this way, but you have lost a daughter. You could have gained another son, but you blew it. Don't come after me. I want nothing to do with you. Anything or anyone that I can think of that might solve this, that information has been handed over to the police department here." Ker grew silent, unable to speak any further.

Brody spoke, his eyes on Ker. "Mrs. Deeks. I know that you sent the men who assaulted me. They wanted Ker to be brought to them. That will never happen. If you come after her again, I will stop you. She is my bride, the love of my life, and I will not tolerate any harm done to her. I am not threatening you. Merely stating that I will cooperate with the authorities in any way that is necessary to prevent that from ever happening."

The screen on her television went black as Ker's mother stared at it. How dare they, she thought once more? She spun, looking for her phone. They had warned her. Warnings never worked. She had too many people that she could call to end this with her daughter.

Only this time, she had been branded by the news story. Everyone that she had used in the past for her dirty deeds refused to answer her call or said they didn't have time to help her. She was growing desperate. The man and woman that she worked for were demanding she provide more children and teenagers. She had never thought of what happened to them. She was just glad for the money that she was accumulating in the bank. Soon, she would have enough to leave Canada and find some island or tropical paradise where she could live. She didn't care that she was leaving death and destruction in her wake.

She paced through the downtown area of Brody's town, looking for an accomplice and finding none. She didn't realize the esteem that the Foundation was held in. No one would go against the Foundation or the men and ladies who lived in the Foundation building.

Dropping down onto a park bench, Ker's mother slumped down, not holding herself in the usual haughty manner that she normally she did. The patrol officer drove past her and then circled the block, leaving his vehicle to stand in front of her.

"Mrs. Deeks? You need to come with me, please." He reached for her hand just as she slammed forward into him. They fell together, the officer rolling her over, and seeing the spreading red stain on the front of her blouse. He frantically tried to stem the flow of blood, calling for help. But she would never face justice on earth. Someone had taken care of that.

Dallas stood, listening to the report, a somber look on his face. He had been part of Brody and Ker's story, standing in the background as they spoke, listening to the reports that were coming in. He shook his head. Now, he had to face Ker and let her know that her mother was dead, murdered, but they were no further ahead in finding the ones responsible for that or who it was her mother worked for.

Brody stood for a moment watching Dallas walk towards him across the lobby. He had been restless and Ker had sent him out for a walk, telling him that he was bothering her and she needed a break. He had looked at her, hurt for a moment, before she reached to hug him.

"I didn't mean it that way, Brody. I'm sorry. I just need a few minutes on my own."

"I understand. I am just oversensitive, I guess. I'll walk into the lobby. That way, you can come to find me if you want me." He walked away, puzzled at her mood. Please, Lord, don't let her do anything that would harm her. She needs to talk to me and I am not sure that she will.

"Brody? You're out and about. Where's Ker?" Dallas stood watching him move not as carefully as he had been. "You're healing."

"I am. Ker needed some space. This is why I am down here. But you have some bad news."

"I do, Brody. I need to learn to school my expressions better. Can we find Ker?"

"You can. I'm right here." Ker's grin lit up her face as Dallas jumped at her voice.

"So you are. Can we sit? It's been a long day already, and my feet are tired." Dallas pointed to one of the sitting areas in the lobby.

"You have bad news. I can tell. What did Mom do now?" Ker barely let him get seated before she spoke.

"I'm sorry, Ker. Your mother was shot earlier today. She didn't make it. One of our officers had found her and had approached her to bring her in for questioning. He didn't see where the assailant was."

"She's dead?" Ker paled, her hands clasped together. "No, it can't be true."

Brody swept her close to him, his eyes on Dallas. "You're sure it was her?"

"We are. I'm so sorry, Ker. I know that this will not bring any closure for you."

"No, it won't. She had to be working for someone, but who? That's who did this." Ker looked up. "I was listed at one point as her next of kin and executrix if Dad couldn't serve. I need to contact her lawyer." She groaned. "And it's the law firm that Dad wanted nothing to do with."

"I can obtain a court order for records, Ker. And if you need to go to that office, I will personally escort you. How be we talk in the morning?"

"That will work, Dallas. Right now, Ker needs some time." Brody reached to shake his friend's hand. "I know this is not easy for you. Call me later."

Chapter 27

Breck looked up as Brendon stopped beside him. He had found a quiet moment or two and had gone to sit in one of the gardens, just to commune with God.

"Brendon? I don't like that face of yours." Breck moved over so that Brendon could sit beside him.

"You'll like what I have to say even less. Ker's mother was killed earlier today."

"She was what?" Breck groaned. "That's not good. Ker knows?"

"She does. Dallas came out himself and talked to them. Brody said that Ker's really quiet right now, not saying much, but she is hurting."

"That she would be. What can we do?" Breck rose, heading back for the building. "The fellows are in the conference room?"

"Those who can be. Ker seems to think that her mother was working for someone else."

"That's been our feeling. How do we prove it?" Breck stood for a moment outside the conference room.

"I have no idea. It only gets worse. Ker is one of the executors, and the lawyer her mother used is the one her father was trying to get away from. Dallas will go with her, he said, whenever she needs to go there.

Both he and Brody are adamant that she's not going anywhere on her own."

"No, she can't. Whoever it is will be waiting for her." Breck began to pace. "How far are we in the search?"

"Far enough along that we've been able to start feeding information to Dallas for him to verify. Emma's been sending us information, but she and Jace are still tied up on that priority case."

"That's good. We need to talk to her brother. How is her father?"

"Still unconscious. Dallas hasn't said much other than that." Brendon held the door open. "I can work for a while before I need to leave." He looked around at the men gathered, somber looks on their faces. He knew that Brody had been in.

"I think that it's time we pulled you all back in for now. Talk to your employers. We may need some of you to head to Ker's hometown."

"We thought of that. Bradon, Benen, and Burnie are heading that way tomorrow. They haven't said anything to Brody, not until they're back."

"My advice is not to hide it from Ker. She will not accept that it was done for her own good."

Brendon nodded. "I'll head up and talk to them. It's hard in this situation to know what to say."

"It is difficult. Let them know that they are in all our prayers."

Brody stepped back from the door, letting Brendon in, early that evening. He had tried to comfort Ker, but she had shut down to some extent. He could relate, he thought, knowing that was how he had reacted all those years ago.

"Brendon? What can I do for you?" Brody pointed towards the kitchen. "I just made a fresh pot of coffee. I won't be going to bed very early, I don't think. I need to try and do some work, but Ker comes first."

Brendon took the mug with a word of thanks before he looked around.

"Where is Ker?"

"In the office. She finally settled down on the couch in there. She's not talking much." Brody studied his friend. "You need to talk to her?"

"With her. And you. If she's up to it."

"Let me see." Brody looked past Brendon. "Ker? Brendon would like to speak with us. You up to it?"

Ker shrugged, her eyes on Brendon. "I don't see why not. Brendon?"

"Three of the fellows are heading to your hometown tomorrow, Ker. They have some information that they need to verify."

"And they can't do it from here. That's what you're saying." Ker sighed. "I'm not sure that they will find any assistance there. They might." Ker studied him. "You're not one of them."

"No, I'm not. Bradon, Benen, and Burnie are." Brendon heard a sound of agreement from Brody but did not take his eyes from Ker.

"Those three?" Ker's shrugged again. "I guess that's what will work. I'm sorry, I can't give any names for them to talk to. I'm just not sure about anyone there now." She rubbed at her temple. "Brody, do you have any pain medications that aren't prescription?"

"I do. Have a seat on the couch, Kitten. I'll find that and some juice for you. Brendon, go on in."

Brendon sank into the chair that he favoured when he visited Brody, his eyes on Ker.

"Ker? What can we do to help you?"

"I really don't know, Brendon. Not anymore. Losing Mom, even though she was responsible for so much damage to people, it's hard. I'll never hear her explanation of what went wrong. Keefe isn't around. And Dad doesn't know what's been happening." She looked up as Brody sat beside her, taking the medication and juice that he handed her. "I'll need to go back there, I think."

"Not necessarily at the moment. We could give authorization to one of the fellows to do whatever it is that you need."

"We could. But I still have to face that lawyer."

"And we will. How deep do you think he's involved?" Brody looked up at a sound from Brendon. "Brendon? What have you not told us?"

"That the lawyer is deeply involved, but we don't think that he's the top man. Dallas is obtaining search warrants for your parents' documents from them. That would save you a trip there, even though as executrix you would have access to your mother's."

"They would do that? They could?" Ker shifted to look up at Brody. "Brody?"

"We'll let Dallas work on it first. Then, if that doesn't work, we'll see, Kitten. Brendon, where are we in the process?"

"Getting there. We need your legal mind down there."

"And he's not going down there. Not for hours at a time." Ker was adamant that he wouldn't. "Bring what you need up here. Maybe, we could work together on it."

"And that would be a great idea." Brendon grinned at Brody as he stared down at his wife.

Chapter 28

Benen stared out the back window of Burnie's car, glad to be leaving the town behind. The three of them had spent the day there. Ker was right, he thought. Not a lot of information was readily available to them. Someone was preventing that. And he wanted to know who.

"What are your thoughts, Bradon?" Burnie finally spoke.

"Ker was right, wasn't she? She certainly knows her town." Bradon paused. "I would have thought someone would have spoken to us."

"Me, too. It's like they have all been threatened. In a town that size, even small as it is, there should have been someone who was willing to break ranks." Benen stuffed his hand into his pocket, and then withdrew it, a frown on his face. "What's this?"

Bradon looked back at him. "What's what?"

"This? It's a note. From someone in town. Asking that we stop in the town mid-way home. Whoever it is, wants to meet us. They have even given instructions as to where. So, do we?"

Bradon shared a look with Burnie. "Who do we know on the police force there?"

"Eric. That's where he is, isn't it?"

"It is." Benen's phone was out, calling Eric. "Eric? Benen. We're fine. And you? Say, are you working today? You're not? Terrific. You know that Brody and Ker are going through some stuff? She did. Okay, here's what's happening. Bradon, Burnie, and I were to Ker's hometown today. Somehow I was passed a note, asking that we meet in your town. At a local business. The EyePatch company." Benen pulled his phone back to stare at it. "It's what? Oh. That's what I thought you said. So, we don't go? You'll go? Okay. Then, we'll keep on driving. Call when you know something."

"Well?" Bradon stared back at Benen as he just sat, turning his phone over and over in his hand.

"Eric said not to go. It's a shady area of town. The business? It's known to be a local drug dealer's but they have never had the evidence to charge anyone. This might be it, he says."

"Home, then. I had to disappoint Ker." Burnie frowned. "Or will we?"

"I don't think so." Benen sighed as he pulled out his phone. "It's Breck. He's called an emergency meeting for tonight with all of us. Something must have come up."

"I would say likely." Bradon grew quiet, his thoughts on their reception in Ker's town. "She knew, didn't she?"

"What's that?" Benen looked up from the research he had been doing.

"Ker knew exactly what would happen."

"She did. She knows her town. But there has to be someone who would be willing to talk to us." Benen was frustrated.

"It depends on how desperate they are or how much they want her town to change." Bradon pulled out his phone. "It's Brody. He wants to know how it went so that he can prepare Ker." He looked at the other two. "What do we tell him?"

Burnie shrugged. "What can we tell him other than it went as Ker told us it would."

Bradon sent off his text, frowning at the response. "Ker asked if we talked to someone named Mary Beth. Did we?"

"I don't remember that name. Where would we have found her?"

"In the library. We were there. I don't remember seeing anyone who had a name tag on with that name."

"Brody said Ker suspects that Mary Beth wasn't there. That it would have been arranged that she wasn't. She's a wealth of information for the town. Ker added that whoever it is that's in charge would keep her from talking with us, somehow, some way."

"I don't like the sounds of that."

"Nor does Brody. He's ready to have this solved. Just like you and I were, Benen."

Burnie frowned at a thought. "She was in the library, right?"

"That's what Ker said."

———

"Only we didn't find her. Now, if she was there and had hidden herself from us, would she take the card that we left on the desk and contact us?"

Benen stared at him. "I forgot we did that. She just might."

Chapter 29

Breck stood at the head of a table in the conference room, his gaze stopping on each of the men gathered there, before he exchanged a look with Barnabas. Bruce and Dallas were there as well. Crucial information had been handed to Dallas, and he had asked if he could meet with the men. He felt it was too important and too life-threatening for both Ker and Brody to let it go another day.

"Thanks for giving me time this evening, fellows. Before we begin, let's pair off and spend some time in prayer. From what I have been told, we are going to need the Lord's guidance and wisdom in this."

Thirty minutes later, the men shifted around to stare back at Breck, who looked up from where he had been talking with Barnabas, Bruce, and Dallas. He sighed. What Dallas would say would rock Brody's world, to put it one way. He was just glad that Bruce was there. They would need his wisdom, he thought, before the night was over.

"Fellows, Dallas approached Bruce and Barnabas late this afternoon. He has come into contact with someone who he has interviewed. That person has provided information that Dallas' team is busy verifying. But the content of it was concerning enough that he felt he had to talk to us. Brody, this directly affects you and Ker. Dallas?" Breck turned to Dallas, who had approached him.

"Fellows, Brody, in particular. I have no words for how I feel right now. It's disheartening and discouraging when you happen upon an informant who provides what they have. Burnie, Benen, and Bradon tell me that they hit a dead end today in Ker's town. Other than a message slipped to Benen. That message he relayed to Eric, who asked that they not stop in his town. The area that they were to meet this person was one of great risk to them. Eric was setting up to watch for this person. He has been asked to contact me if and when that person shows.

"Now, the informant that came forward is from our town. I will not give any more details than that. This person was known to Ker's mother and the ones over her. We have been provided with information that directly ties her to the abduction and disappearance of a number of children and teens. Given the names and details, our team is frantically working with the child welfare unit of the social services and the child and teen exploitation section of our department. We have no idea how long this has been going on, but we feel it has been for at least twenty years. Ker would have been a young child when it started. Keefe, just older.

"Now, as to Keefe? We are keeping him apart from Ker. Some of what he has been stating is contradictory to what Ker has said, and more in line with what their mother said. We need to verify if he is telling us the truth and if he is involved in the crimes or not. I pray that he is not. Ker needs her brother." Dallas paused to sip from his water bottle, his eyes on Brody, who was staring at the pad of paper in front of him, his pen moving rapidly.

———

"Dallas? Are you confident in what you say about Keefe?" Brendon spoke up.

"We are, unfortunately. We are going back over all his trips and vacations, trying to determine if they coincided with any of the disappearances. So far, they haven't. Pray that he is not involved."

"Her father?" Bradon asked. "Has he awakened and been able to talk?"

"He has. He fatigues easily, as you can imagine, but he is willing to talk as much as he can. He didn't see who it was who struck him. He is concerned about Ker. That was his first statement when he was coherent enough to be understood."

"So, calling Brody was deliberate on his part?" Brady studied his friend, Brody, watching him intently.

"It was. He told the investigators who spoke with him that he had been warned that she would disappear the next day or else die. He arranged for Brody to appear, hoping that Ker would go with him. If she hadn't, he had plans to move her from their town. Only, we know what happened." Dallas turned for a moment as Bruce spoke quietly with him.

Dallas' face grew grim as he nodded, his eyes finding Brody.

"Brody, Bruce would like to speak with you in private and then speak with Ker. We'll catch you up on what else we discuss. Buckley?"

———

Buckley nodded as he rose, following Bruce and Brody from the room, the eyes of their friends following them.

"Bruce? What is that important that you pull me from the meeting?"

"Brody, I have no words to tell you. Ker's father passed away just a short while ago. He had undiagnosed heart disease and had a heart attack."

Brody paled, staggering from the shock, Buckley's hand there to hold him upright. "How do I tell her?" His voice was a mere whisper. "How do I tell her that her father is gone before she could see him again?"

Chapter 30

Brody found Ker on the balcony outside his home office, wrapped in a blanket as she sat, staring at the night sky, counting the stars as much as she could. She loved clear nights like this one was. She felt closer to God when she could see the stars. She leaned into his hug, surprised to see him home so soon.

"Brody? Is your meeting over already?"

"Not really. Bruce was there and needed to speak with us. He and Buckley are waiting in the living room for us."

Ker searched his face, seeing the sadness in it. "Which one?" Her voice was barely a whisper.

"Which one?" Brody echoed her words, trying to find his own words to tell her.

"Which one? Dad? Keefe? And how?" She felt herself hugged tightly before Brody drew her to her feet.

"Bruce wants to tell you." He shut the door quietly behind them and reached for her hand, a prayer audible to only the two of them, before he led her towards the living room.

Ker hesitated as she saw Bruce and Buckley stand. "Bruce? Buckley? Brody said that you needed to speak with me."

"I do, Ker. You may want to sit first." Bruce watched with compassion as she sat on the edge of a chair, Brody perching on the arm, holding her to him.

"Bruce? Which one? Dad or Keefe?" Her eyes searched his, seeing the truth in his. "Dad?"

"It was your father, Ker. Did you know he had heart disease?"

"No, not really. He had seen the doctor about six weeks ago. He wouldn't say why, but I suspected something like that. Is that what happened?"

"I'm sorry, Ker, but he had a heart attack. He was alert enough before that to speak with the investigators. His first thought was for you."

Ker drew in a trembling breath, her fingers pushing about her lips to try and stem the tears. "It was?"

"It was. Dallas has spoken with them. Your father confirmed that he brought Brody in to meet with you, in the hopes that he would convince you to leave. If he hadn't, your father had made alternate plans. If you had not left, then you would have disappeared the next day."

"Mom?"

"That's what he implied. He didn't come right out and say it."

"No, he wouldn't. He never laid blame, not unless he had absolute proof. And he wouldn't have had with Mom." She sighed. "Now, what?"

"Now, we work with you on your duties for the estate. Our lawyers have met and one of them will work with you. We are familiar with the firm you indicated has your parents' paperwork. There will be no issues retrieving it."

"There won't? I thought there would be." Ker shared a look with Brody.

"Bruce means that the lawyers will know better than to try anything. The Foundation lawyers will not allow it. If I know them, they will have what they need to convince them to cooperate or they will face a hearing with the law society."

"Brody is correct, Ker. They are already on the radar of the law society. A new complaint that is substantiated would mean they would lose their licenses. And they won't want to do that."

They spoke for a while longer before Bruce looked at Buckley, who nodded.

"Ker, in situations like this, our church works with the families. You are family to the Foundation and to the church, even if you are a new member. We want to do what we can to help you get through this. Brody, when you need to make any arrangements, talk to me. Right now, Ker needs to absorb what she has been told and to begin to grieve. Let me pray with you, and then we're on our way. Ker, I meant it. Call at any time. That's what our church family does."

Brody walked slowly back from the door after the two men had left, not quite sure how to approach Ker. He found her in the kitchen, the kettle plugged in as she watched it boil, his coffee perking in the pot beside it. His arm around her, he just stood, unable to find the words that he needed.

"Brody?"

"Yes, my love?"

"I didn't get to say goodbye to either one of my parents. It's so not right."

"No, it's not. We have some decisions to make. Dallas will be in touch with Keefe. Do you need to talk to him?"

Ker shrugged. "Right at the moment? No. I've been remembering things that I shoved to the back of my mind. Was he involved?"

"That's what we are surmising, but it may be false information that we have been given."

"That's true." Ker sighed as she turned into his hug. "I will need to speak with him, but I don't want him around me. Not if it's unproven. But he has to be, doesn't he?"

"He does. But I can guarantee you that you will have your own bodyguards. Each one of the fellows will be close enough to that he can't try anything."

"And if I'm wrong about him? How do I ask him to forgive me?" She turned as she heard her phone chime. Her face paled as she read the text.

"Ker?" Brody reached for her phone, his own face growing stern. "This is Keefe's number?"

"It is. And only he could be on his phone unless he unlocked it for someone. He is involved, isn't he?"

Chapter 31

A day later, Ker looked up from where she was sitting in the lobby, finding Devaney, Ennis, and Fynn approaching her. Fynn handed over a mug of tea before she sat, her feet curled under her.

"Ker? We've been looking for you. We haven't had a chance to gossip in a few days." Fynn grinned at her.

"Gossip? Fynn! You know that we don't gossip." Ennis shook a finger at her friend.

"You know what I mean! We talk, we discuss, we get to know one another. We learn secrets that some people don't want to share."

Devaney laughed. "And that would be my secret that you're trying to find out, is it, Fynn? Not telling."

Ker stared at them all. "You gossip? I didn't think you ladies did."

"We gossip, but in a nice way. We never tear anyone down. When we gossip with one another, it is to try and build up each other. It's our form of gossip." Ennis laughed at the expression on Ker's face. "We have confused you."

"No, I get what you are saying. I just have never heard it expressed that way. And you three are so happy. Even with what you went through."

"We are, Ker. God has been good. We are blessed with husbands who love and adore us. We have a huge family here that loves us. They tolerate our nonsense, the fellows do, but we do the same for them." Ennis watched her closely. "Tell us, Ker. What can we do for you? We have been praying for you."

"Thank you. I needed that." Ker blinked away the tears of thankfulness. "I have never had such prayers as you ladies send forth. It's just so normal and natural for you to talk like that. That is how I've always thought we should be. But I was never allowed to do that. That's what I think I have been searching and seeking for. That freedom."

"You've come to the right place then, Ker." Devaney reached to hug her. "We have all had to learn over time to do just that. It has not been easy at times." She searched Ker's face. "Now, talk to us. You need to tell us what is going on. We can give you a female perspective on what you're enduring."

"Enduring?" Fynn began to laugh. "Devaney! You and your expressions. You have gotten worse over time."

Devaney smirked. "I know I have. It's called growth."

Ker began to laugh. "I needed that, Devaney. You don't know how much. Now, as to what is going on? Where do I start?"

"At the beginning, but I think we've already done that." Ennis laughed at the expression on her face. "What can you tell us?"

Fynn pulled out her ever-present notepad and pen. "And I will take notes. They may be too scientific for you though." She frowned at her pen.

"It's not the pen's fault, Fynn. It's how your brain works. Ker, this lady was in college at age 16, graduated with her degrees and doctorate at age 20, and went right to work in a medical examiner's office. She was one of those who went in and studied the creepy crawlies at a crime scene."

"You were? Oh, that sounds fascinating." Ker looked with new interest at Fynn. "I still haven't made it to your building."

"You will. Brody will make sure. Now, where do you stand?"

"I'm not, I'm sitting." Ker smirked at the laughter. "Seriously? With Mom and Dad gone, it's put a lot of pressure on me. The lawyers here are handling a lot of it. Brody drew up papers and had me sign them. For some reason, Keefe had never been named to an executor position."

"That is strange. But go on." Ennis pushed her to continue.

Ker explained where they stood in the investigation, as much as she could reveal, and then listened to the ladies discuss it. She shifted over as Hagen sat, reaching to take Hagen's daughter from her even as Ennis reached for Hagen's son. Ker cuddled the little girl close, her hand rubbing her back, not even realizing how she was acting like a mother.

———

"So, with your brother, Ker, what's going on?" Hagen had listened to the update from Fynn.

"I'm not sure. Dallas isn't saying." She sighed. "I thought I had a brother I could depend on, but now I'm not so sure."

"What if he's being set up? Would your mother have put something like that into play?" Fynn looked up, a distracted look on her face. "I have seen that on some of the cases I worked on."

"You did?" Ker hesitated, a finger rubbing at her temple. "I wondered that. I don't know who the investigators are but I wonder if they had been gotten to? That they're feeding Dallas information that's not from Keefe? The brother I know and love would not be acting like this." She paused, her lips compressing even as anger sparked for a moment in her eyes. "Dad sent Keefe away. Would he have done that if Keefe had been involved? Mom would say Keefe had done and said things, things that didn't seem to be him. I never fully believed them."

"Where is he?" Fynn looked up again.

"I don't know exactly. He has been texting me, and Brody and I have been responding."

"Then, we look at the cell records. Emma will help." Ennis had her phone out, sending a text message off to Emma, and smiling at the quick response. "Emma had thought of that and has obtained the records. Her husband and his team are bringing Keefe back today."

"They are? And just who are they?" Ker was confused.

"Emma and Abe are friends. They have helped out some of us. Emma finds people and information that no one else seems to be able to. Abe has a security team. They do training mainly now, but they do go in and bring out people that need rescuing."

"They do? Abe? That name sounds familiar." Ker looked around, surprised to see all the ladies had crowded around. "Oh my, when did you all get here?"

"Over the length of time that you have been here." Cadee grinned. "And we brought lunch. Brody has been told to stay away, that this is our time with you. You need some time with the ladies."

Ker began to laugh, waving at Brody as he watched from near the stairs. "And he's standing guard, you know."

"We know." Berneen smirked. "He's in love, Ker. And he wants this over for you." She tilted her head and watched as Ker blushed. "And Ker's in love." Her voice had softened. "We are so happy for you two. Brody is a wonderful man, and you two are just right for each other."

Chapter 32

Brody watched as Brennen paced the conference room, not quite sure what was up. He looked around as the door behind him opened, and then he was on his feet, his hand outstretched to shake that of the man who appeared.

"Abe Findlay? What are you doing here?"

"Looking for you. And I understand that you are married. Congratulations. I would like to meet your wife." Abe studied Brody carefully, seeing the bruises that were fading, but the stress that was showing on his face.

"Sure. We can head up now if you like."

"I would like." Abe waved at the few men who were gathered in the room and looked up as he left.

"You're here for a reason, Abe. I know you that well."

"I am, Brody. That reason is why I need to speak with your wife." Abe waited in the hallway of the apartment as Brody searched for Ker.

Ker studied the man waiting, a frown on her face before it cleared.

"Tell me? You're Abe?"

"That I am. You have guessed well." Abe grinned at her.

"The ladies and I were talking. Someone said that you had become involved. Tell me. Did you find Keefe?"

"We did. We have him at our place, for now, Ker, just until we clear him to come this way. Can we sit? This will take a while."

"Sure. Have you eaten? I have sandwiches and soup ready." Ker looked worried for a moment.

"Sandwiches and soup are just fine, Ker. What can I do to help?"

"Just have a seat. Brody?"

"On it, Kitten. Here, you sit for a change. I'll dish it up." Brody worked quickly, setting their meal in place and then sitting himself beside Ker, reaching for her hand. "Abe, will you?"

"I would be glad to." Abe's prayer covered more than just their meal and left the younger couple refreshed and confident that they could handle what he would tell them.

"Abe?" Ker finally pushed her meal away. "How is Keefe?"

"Not in great shape. Whoever said the police had him in protective custody lied. There is no other word for it. He was not in police custody. Whoever it was that Dallas was speaking with has to be involved in this. We have passed the names on to our own police detectives. We have a friend who will assess him and treat him. For now, we'll keep you two apart. I understand that you are planning the funerals for your parents. We will make sure he's here for those if this is not resolved by that time."

"And you think it might be?" Brody was hopeful.

"It may well be, Brody. Emma has been finding a wealth of information, between her and Jace. Dallas is pleading with her to slow down, but you know Emma. She can't. It's not in her to do that."

"No, it's not. What can you tell us or can you?"

"Emma is the best one to do that. She wants to head this way in two days. She states that she needs that time to confirm some information she's finding. We'll head back here then if it's convenient for you two."

"Any time is convenient." Ker was indignant. "And not soon enough."

"Wow, Ker. Tell me off or what!" Abe was laughing. "You sound like some of the ladies my men are married to. They all had adventures, just like you two, and so did Emma and I. Don't worry. We will keep you updated as much as we can between now and then. Now, if I may take the time to pray for you two once more, I need to get on the road. I have a training session scheduled for early tomorrow."

"And yet you came here tonight." Ker grew silent, her eyes on Brody. "Will you give Keefe a message for me? Will you tell him that I love him? That I miss my big brother?"

"I can do that. If tomorrow he's coherent enough, I will have a call set up for you. May I have your phone number?" Abe took the slip of paper from her and tucked it into his pocket before he rose.

Brody walked him to the door. "Thank you, Abe. That's a relief for us, knowing Keefe is not involved."

"I am sure it is. We'll find out who it is. Emma already has an idea and has been in touch with Dallas tonight, she said.

Chapter 33

Ker stared down at her phone. She had just spoken with Abe's wife, Emma, who had called just to say hello and ask how she was. That surprised Ker. She had never had that before. She looked up as Brody's hand rested on her head for a moment before he stooped to kiss her.

"You okay?" His voice was quiet.

"I am. I just spoke with Emma. Did you know that she just called to see how I was?"

"That would be Emma. With Keefe at their place or with one of their friends, she would want to make sure that you are okay with it all." Brody sat beside her, reaching for her phone that she had clutched in her hands and dropping it onto the coffee table.

"It's nice, you know? What have I missed all my life, Brody?" Ker turned to him, finding him watching her intently.

"I don't know that you have missed a lot, Ker. You have missed out on friendships, but you likely missed out on heartaches too."

Ker reached for her phone as it chimed, her face paling at the number. "This is Mom's phone number. Who has her phone?"

Brody reached for his phone, trying to reach Dallas and having to leave a voice mail for him. "Dallas will call us back. I'll let him deal with that."

"Do you think Keefe was involved?" Ker's voice showed that she was hopeful he hadn't been.

"From what we can find out, I don't think so. Emma's fed us a lot of information that we're collating with what we have. Dallas is also copied on everything. I don't think Keefe was. It just doesn't seem to be his character, not from what we have learned."

"That's a relief." Ker snuggled down against him. "Where do we go from here, Brody?"

"With this? I am not sure. The fellows are working it as a huge logic problem."

Ker laughed. "A logic problem? Do they have a diagram and all?"

"They do. It's posted on the wall in the conference room."

"I need to see it. Will they let me?"

"They would never dream of stopping you. How be we head on down there?" Brody waited for Ker to move but she didn't. He tilted his head to look at her and then smiled. She was asleep, just like that. He had heard her pacing the apartment during the night for the last few days. He simply held her and prayed for his lady.

An hour later, Ker stirred, rubbing at her nose and face, before she looked up at him, finding that he was asleep as well. She gave a small smile and then reached for her phone, scrolling through her messages. Some she erased. Some she saved. Some she forwarded to Dallas, those ones scaring her. And then there was one from Keefe. It was not a phone number that she recognized, but Abe had said that would be the case. She smiled sadly as she read it, knowing there were just the two of them left in their family.

Brody had roused, his eyes on Ker as she worked away.

"Ker?"

"I'm okay, sweetheart. It's just a message from Keefe." She blinked away the tears. "He misses me, he says. And he says Abe will be calling us."

"And he will. That I know from experience. If he says he is calling, Abe will." He looked over her shoulder. "And there's a message from him, isn't it?"

"There is. He's heading this way tomorrow with Emma. I wonder if Keefe will come as well."

"It depends on how he is. Abe will bring him if he feels it's safe enough. Whoever was holding him will be watching you, just to see if Keefe is in touch."

"I know they will. Can we go downstairs now, Brody? I want to be part of this now. The lawyers are working on the estate for me. Bruce arranged that."

"I know he did. Here, let's go then, Kitten."

Her hand tucked tight in his, Ker stood just inside the conference room doorway, watching the men at work. She was surprised to see all of them there.

"They're all here!"

"They are. Breck called us all in to work on this." His finger touched her lips as she opened her mouth to protest. "It's what we do, Kitten. We work like this. We have for everyone else."

"I see." Ker moved away from him, wandering the room, stopping to speak with each of the men, before she walked to study the papers on the wall, a finger out on occasion to trace something. Burnie followed her, taking notes as she commented on something before she looked up at the huge puzzle they had placed there.

"A logic puzzle, Burnie? What made you think of that?"

He shrugged. "I have no idea. I used it in a book at one point. This just seemed to fit one of them."

"I can see that." Ker studied what they had written and discarded. "What's this? This name?"

"That name? That's a name and occupation that crossed our desks. We're not sure who it is."

"It's the man who is in charge of the homeless shelter in my town. It has always been rumoured that he was on the take, as they say, but no one could prove it." Ker paled. "He would be perfect for helping people disappear, now wouldn't he?"

"He would, Ker. He's just one that Dallas is looking at." He stepped away for a moment, a thought crossing his mind that he needed to look at.

———

Baird approached her. "Ker? What can we do for you?"

"For me? You're doing so much." She looked surprised. "Why would you ask that?"

"Because it's what we do, Ker. We look after one another." He shared a look with Brody who was standing behind Ker. "Brody?"

"Thanks, Baird. Knowing that you are praying for us as we seek to find the answers not only on this but on what Ker has been missing all her life helps."

Ker suddenly swayed, her face paling as she did so. Brody reached to swing her into his arms, finding the chair suddenly shoved behind him.

"Ker?"

"I remember!" Ker looked up at Brody, her face growing even paler. "I remember him. He and Mom used to talk at church. I wasn't supposed to hear, but I did. Once when I was young. He was talking about someone who had disappeared. He and Mom knew where they were. She mentioned it. I don't know if Dad ever found that boy."

"Do you remember the name?" Brendon crouched down beside her.

"No, I don't. Brody, this is getting worse and worse." Ker looked up at the men who had surrounded her. "We need to stop this, and now. But how?"

"We're working on it, Ker. I know that we keep saying it, but it's the truth." Brendon looked around. "I don't know about anyone else, but this is frustrating to no end for Ker and Brody. What are we missing?"

Ker was on her feet, moving quickly to a blank sheet of paper on the wall, a pen in her hand. She wrote swiftly, listing names, occupations, relationships between them. She moved to a new piece of paper and began to list names of missing children and teens that she knew of. Where they had disappeared. If they had been found and where.

Finally stepping back into the circle of Brody's arms, she studied the wall, fatigue weighing her down.

"Does this help?"

"It does, Ker. We were remiss not to have you in here before. I guess that we were trying to spare you any more distress." Bradon looked worried.

"It's okay, Bradon. I know why you fellows did what you did. Now, if this is what helps, I will do it again and again until we find the ones at the top."

Chapter 34

Standing in front of Ker the next day, Bruce and one of the Foundation lawyers, John Timms, watched as she sagged for a moment and then straightened back up, a determined look on her face. John had been instrumental in obtaining all the paperwork from the other law firm and had been dismayed at what he had found.

"Can we go somewhere and talk this over, Ker?" Bruce looked past her to see Brody heading their way. "Here's Brody."

"Bruce? John?" Brody's voice held the question that he wouldn't ask.

"We just asked that we speak with Ker. I'm glad you're here, Brody." Bruce pointed towards the office that he had in the building.

Ker sat, her hands clasped together, her eyes on the men. "Bruce? What did you find?"

"John will explain. First, we need to pray, Ker. That's how we start our meetings."

Bruce watched with interest as Ker took each document that she was handed, reading it through thoroughly, making notes, asking the questions that he would have expected Brody to ask. Then he realized that he was selling her short, that perhaps they all had been. In front of him was an intelligent, knowledgeable young lady.

"Brody? What is this?" Ker finally held the last paper.

Brody peered at it. "It's a power of attorney for financial affairs."

"But it's not Mom or Dad. Who is this person?"

"It's not?" John reached for it. "You're right. We found that with the paperwork. I needed to speak with you about that one. Do you recognize the name?"

Ker shook her head. "No, I don't. Who is this Ted Lowe?"

"That's what we will look into then, Ker. I think that we have covered everything we need to at present." John shared a look with Brody.

Ker walked away from the meeting with a handful of documents, Brody by her side. He watched her intently, not seeing the distress that he had expected.

"You okay, Kitten?"

"I am, sweetheart. I am. I think that overnight I came to the realization that I cannot change what happened in the past. I cannot change who she was or what she did. I am responsible only for myself. That is something I think I was seeking, to be responsible for others. And I can't be."

"That's good. Prayers are being answered then." He unlocked their apartment door and headed for his office. "Bring your paperwork back here when you're ready. I need to check on my emails. Then, if you want, we can do some research." Brody reappeared when Ker didn't respond. "Ker?"

Ker looked up, a puzzled look on her face. "That name. That Ted Lowe? I don't know it. I'm just not sure why Mom would have had that document."

Brody walked back to her, taking the documents and dropping them on the hallway table, and simply enveloping her into a hug.

"We'll figure it out. Right now? Come with me. You can sit and watch me work." He smirked at the playful swat she aimed his way.

"I need to find something to do, Brody. But with this hanging over me, I don't want to put anyone in danger."

"We get that, Kitten. We'll find something for you. What about going back to school?"

Ker shook her head. "I don't think so." She reached for the documents that he was holding. "Go. Do what you need to. I plan on reading back through these."

An hour later, Brody looked up, a smile creasing his face as he watched Ker. She had stretched out on the couch, dropping the documents to the floor, and was fast asleep. He rose, covering her with a blanket and dropping a kiss on her cheek before he reached for the documents and returned to the desk.

Brody was puzzled as he read through them again, knowing that Ker would not mind him doing just that. He made his own notes, reading hers and her questions. She's good a logical mind, he thought. He stopped at the last document, the one naming her mother as power of attorney for Ted Lowe. He reached instead for his mouse, waking up his computer, and then was deep into research. He didn't like that he could find no evidence of anyone by that name. Sitting back, Brody finally reached for his phone, sending off a request to Emma. She was back to him promptly, promising to have something as soon as she could.

He looked up as he felt a hand on his shoulder. Ker stood there, watching him. He simply reached around and drew her down on his knee, startling her for a moment, before she leaned against him.

"Ker?"

"Brody? What did Mom do? Who is that person?"

"Emma's looking into for us. Did you hear from her or Abe how Keefe is?"

Ker shook her head, a sad look covering her face. "No, and I wish I did. This is so distressing, Brody. I want to move on with our lives, but how can we?"

"We will. We will not let this stop us. Now, how be we head into town for dinner? I would like to take my sweetheart out for a meal?"

"Casual, I hope. I have no dress-up clothes."

"No, you don't, but we'll take care of that. Casual works for me." He watched her face for a moment. "Something is puzzling you."

"There is, Brody, and I don't know how to ask. Am I really your sweetheart?" Ker watched him.

"You are, my love. That you are. You were the one I was waiting for." He kissed her and kissed her again.

Ker sat for a moment, her eyes on him before she spoke. "I am glad, Brody. We need to talk about so much, but with this hanging over us, it just doesn't seem right."

"No, and you are grieving as well." He set her on her feet and rose, his hands reaching for hers. "Come. Let's go do something fun."

Chapter 35

The next morning, Brendon stood at Brody's door, knocking and waiting for an answer. He frowned. He had talked to Brody last the afternoon before and had made plans to meet him that morning. It was not like Brody to not be there.

A thought had him running for the stairs and then to the parking lot, sliding to a stop. No, Brody's truck was not there. Now, where was he? His phone out, Brendon searched for messages and found not.

"Brendon? You look lost." Brady approached him, on his way home from his shift.

"I am. I was to meet with Brody and Ker this morning. There is no answer at their apartment. And his truck is missing." Brendon spun in a circle. "He hasn't parked anywhere else."

Brady shifted his duffel bag and motioned to the building. "Let's head in there. See what we can find. When did you last speak with him?"

"Late yesterday afternoon. He said something about going out for dinner with Ker. I would have thought that they would be back."

Both men turned as they heard their names called and found Abe running towards them.

"Brendon. Brady. Where's Brody? We've been trying to reach him."

"We can't find him. The last I spoke with him was yesterday afternoon." Brendon pulled open the door, waiting for the other two men to enter. "You're here for a reason."

"My whole team is. Emma got word last night that someone would try and kidnap them. Don't tell me that we're too late." Abe was worried. It was not often that Emma received such messages but when she did, they were always correct.

Brady dropped his bag by the elevators and ran towards the office hallway, searching for Breck.

"Breck? Do you have your key for Brody's?"

"I do." Breck looked up from his desk and was on his feet. "Why?"

"We can't find them. Abe's here. There is word that they were to be kidnapped last night."

"What?" Breck moved rapidly, grabbing the keys to the building suites from his desk drawer. "You're sure they're not around?"

"No answer Brendon says at their apartment. And his truck is missing."

"I don't like that, Brady. I was just about to head up there anyway." Breck peered at Abe. "And Abe is here."

"He has his whole team, Breck. Emma sent them."

"She did? That's not good." Breck took the stairs two at a time and landed in front of Brody's apartment in no time. Hearing no answer, he unlocked the door and cautiously opened it, walking through to search. "Not here. Wait. Here's a note. It's from Brody. Now, how did he know to leave one?"

"What does it say?" Abe stood near the open door.

"Just that they were going out for dinner last night. And that they expected to be back by 7. But he had a meeting early this morning. Brendon? Do you know anything about that?"

"No. He had planned to be here." Brendon reached for his phone as it chimed. "This is strange. A message from Brody's phone, but it's not phrased as he would phrase it. Just that he's running late and would be here shortly."

"No, that's not quite how he would phrase it." Breck left the apartment, locking the closed door behind him. "Now where would they have gone?"

"I would suspect somewhere casual." Brady looked around. "Fynn said that Ker has not yet replaced her dress clothes. Was reluctant to in fact. She felt it too much like what her mother had demanded of her."

"Okay, so casual. But that leaves a lot of restaurants." Abe stood for a moment, studying the sky from where he now stood in the parking lot. "We didn't get a lot of information last night. Emma was still trying to confirm it or track down the source and was having difficulty doing that." He looked around as he heard footsteps. "Micah?"

———

"Emma called. She didn't want to call you. She found them."

"She has? Where?" Breck pointed towards his vehicle. "Where do we go?"

"You don't. You three stay here. Let us go in." Abe ran for the SUV, Micah on his heels.

The three watched them drive away, not quite sure what had happened.

"Now what, Breck?" Brady walked back towards the building and inside, retrieving his duffel bag, a yawn catching him unawares.

"We work hard to try and find out who is behind it. Brendon? You had needed to talk to Brody and Ker?"

"I had. I came across another name that I needed to run by them. A Tom Light."

"Tom Light? That's a strange name."

"I know. We have documents on him. Dallas has that information as well." Brendon sighed. "This just does not get any easier."

"It never does. What else?" Breck pulled up a chair at the table that Brendon had claimed.

"Not a lot from what we had last night. I feel like we are missing one small piece and that piece is what we need to crack this wide open."

"I know. Has Ker talked to her brother?"

"Not that I am aware of." Brendon frowned. "I thought that was why Abe was here."

"Obviously not." Breck rubbed at his forehead. "I just wish we could figure it out, fellows. This is wearing on Ker. She's grieving in so many ways, but can't fully and opening grieve or attend the funerals without resolution of it."

Chapter 36

Standing sheltered partway by Brody, Ker stared at the man standing in front of them. She didn't know him, but he looked familiar. Brody refused to let her move past him, his eyes searching for anyone else that was around.

"I just need to talk with you two. That's all." The man was pleading, desperation on his face.

"And why?" Brody was stern, not willing to show how scared he was for Ker.

"Her mother did me wrong. I just want to tell her what happened. There were others as well. I want them brought to justice." The man rubbed at his face, the sound of his hand scraping across his face loud in the stillness of the early night.

"Okay. Brody, where can we meet him that has people around? An all-night coffee shop or cafe?"

"There's one. Just down the road. Lee's. We'll meet you there in thirty minutes. Be on your own."

"I will be. I want to give her some stuff." The man whirled and was gone before either one of the young couples could respond.

"Brody?" Ker was frightened.

"I know, Kitten. I know. That's why I suggested Lee's. He's a friend and works overnight. There are usually patrol officers stopping in for coffee or a meal.

It's the safest place that I can think of." He led her to his truck, tucking her inside, watching for anyone who might approach.

Parking behind the restaurant, Brody took Ker's hand as he walked towards the back door, keying in a code, and then pulling the door open. They stood, just inside the door, watching the activity before Brody pointed to a young man around their age.

"Lee?" Brody's voice was quiet, but the man still spun.

"Brody! Where have you been? You haven't been in for a few days. And just who is this that you're holding onto so tightly?"

"Lee, this is Ker, my bride."

"You're married?" Lee looked surprised before his brows lowered and his eyes narrowed. "Don't tell me. You're having one of those things you call an adventure." He waited for Brody to speak. "You're not saying anything, Brody."

"You told me not to tell you." Brody laughed, Ker's gaze flickering between the two men. "Listen, someone approached us about what we're going through. He's to meet us here. Watch for us, will you?"

"That I can do. Stay here as long as you want. Paul and Peter will be in and out all night. They're on duty."

"That's good." Brody hesitated. "I just want you to watch and see if anyone is around that shouldn't be."

"On it, Brody. You've done a lot for my family, you and the Foundation people." Lee pointed to a corner booth. "Take the one I usually use. I can see you from here. Coffee for you. Ker? May I call you that? I can? Oh, terrific. Tea?"

"Thank you, Lee. I would appreciate that." Ker was quiet as she seated herself on the bench seat and slid over for Brody to sit on the outside. "What are we expecting, Brody?"

"I have no idea. He seemed almost too eager to talk to us."

"I know. That scares me." Ker watched as the man entered the diner, looked around, and then headed their way. "Here we go, Brody. Do we need to let anyone else know?"

The man hesitated before he sat, looking up as Lee approached with coffees for the men and tea for Ker.

"Anything else?"

"Have you eaten today?" Brody watched with compassion as the man finally shook his head. "Lee, bring us a meal for him. For me, a piece of whatever pie you have. Ker?"

"Nothing for me, thank you, unless you have some fresh fruit?"

"I do. I'll be back with some for you." Lee walked away, to stand where he could not be seen and could watch the man. "Peter? Have you seen him before?"

Peter, Lee's brother and a patrol officer, stood behind him. "I have. He's been wandering around the downtown area for the last couple of days. He seems harmless but we're watching him." Peter looked around. "I'm off duty soon. I'll change to street clothes and come back."

"Thanks. Brody and Ker are going through something.'

"Ker? That's her with him? She's a beauty."

"She is. She and Brody are married."

"Where do they find all these beautiful women?" Peter was happily married but liked to tease Lee, who was still single.

"I have no idea, but ten of them have." He turned. "Let me know when you're back."

"I will. Watch yourself."

Lee set the meal down in front of the man, seeing his trembling hand as he reached for the fork, pausing as Brody prayed for the food.

"No one has done that for me for years. Thank you."

"Okay, eat. Then, we talk." Brody sipped at his coffee, even as Ker ate her fruit, both of them watchful.

"Now, tell me. What did you want to talk to us about?" Ker finally spoke, her eyes on the man.

"I know you. I saw you with her."

"With who?"

"Your mother, I think. She wanted me to do something and I wouldn't. Then she stole from me. I just want to know why."

Chapter 37

Brody was surprised at what he heard, but then he realized that he shouldn't have been. What they had discovered over the last few days was that Kelly Deeks in fact did steal from people. Not just in money but in identification and documents. It was disconcerting, to say the least. Ker had just looked at them as they had detailed it all and shrugged. To her, it was just who her mother had been and become.

"Why would you say that?" Ker pushed.

"Because it's what she did best. She stole from people. She took my identity and used it for someone else. That ruined me. She stole who I was." The man reached carefully into his pocket and pushed across an envelope. "My name is Lowe. Your pa was kind to me when I met him. I was looking for work, hadn't worked in months. He set me up with a friend of his to do landscaping. I was happy there until your mother came around. She kept after me to do dirty deeds for her. I owed her, she would say. I said no, I didn't owe her or anyone. What I had, I had worked for.

"She kept after me. I finally had to leave town, but when I did, I found that my identification was gone. I had to replace it. She forged a power of attorney using my name and gave it to someone, some lawyer I think it was. I tried to get it, but I couldn't prove that it was fake. I went to the police but they just laughed at me and threatened to put me in jail." The man paused, his jaw working as he tried to control his emotions.

"So then, what happened?" Brody shared a look with Ker, even as he tried to watch the people in the cafe. He nodded at Lee and Peter as they moved around the main portion of the building.

"So, I had to start all over, in another town. I went to a lawyer there, and we managed to stop her. But it didn't help my reputation. I had to rebuild it all. I watched her from afar, just waiting for an opportunity to bring her to justice. I didn't want revenge, but I didn't want her to do to someone else what she had done to me." Lowe paused. "She ran with some pretty bad people. I would see them with kids and teens and then hear that they had disappeared. I tried to follow her one day. Someone must have seen me. I ended up in the hospital with a broken leg from being run down in a parking lot."

Ker looked down at the envelope. "What's in here?"

"As much evidence as I could find. It also has my statements from the police about what happened and when. I kept it, hoping to find you or your brother. Your father? I was never sure about him."

"Dad wasn't involved." Ker looked up at Brody. "Keefe? We don't think he was."

"He wasn't. Your mother made sure that you kids weren't. At least, not directly. I overheard her threaten you two about four months ago. She was speaking with your pa."

"That's about the time Dad became more distracted. Brody, did he know?"

"I would suspect so. Lowe, what else?" Brody nodded as Lee held up the coffee carafe. "Here, Lee. Refill this for Lowe. Would you like anything?"

Lowe hesitated and Brody shared another look with Lee.

"It's okay. Have want you want. It's on the house." Lee nodded as Lowe looked up in surprise. "So, what kind of pie would you like?" He just grinned at Lowe.

Two hours later, Ker had finally given in to her fatigue and cradled her head on her folded arms and slept. Lee had arrived with the plaid blanket that he kept in his office and handed it to Brody to cover her. The men's conversation had drifted to many things, coming back time and again to God. Brody rubbed at his sore eyes, but he refused to give in. There was something about Lowe, that made him want to trust him, even though he still wasn't sure of him.

"What do you plan to do now?" Brody turned his spoon over and over, not looking at the other man.

"Move on, I guess. Try and find somewhere that I can live until I can retire. If I can even do that." Lowe sighed. "I regret this. I trusted her pa."

"And your trust was broken not by him. Do you like this area?"

"I do. I moved around the province after my wife died. She was young and had cancer. I just couldn't stay in one place, grieving too hard, I guess. This has felt like home."

"Then, don't move on. Have you heard of the Barnabas Foundation?"

Lowe stared at him. "Who in this area hasn't? They're good people. Take care of people." He was puzzled. "Why?"

"Because I work for them. I am also a paralegal. Let us help you. I want to solve whatever it is that needs solved for my wife. And her brother. I can talk to them. See where we can find you work and a home. In the meantime, try the shelter here. Another one of the Foundation men's in-laws run it. Just tell them Brody sent you. They'll take you in." He nodded at the lightening sky. "It's almost dawn. Why don't we spend some time in prayer, my friend?"

Lowe blinked rapidly as his emotions caught the best of him. "You would do that for a stranger? For someone who might have harmed you or your woman?"

"I would. You're a brother in Christ. I can do no less than give you a helping hand."

Chapter 38

It was early morning, the breakfast rush just starting, when Ker roused, blinking to clear her vision. She frowned for a moment.

"We're still in the diner?"

"We are, Kitten. Have a good sleep?" Brody just grinned at her.

"I guess. Where's Lowe?"

"He's gone. I sent him to the shelter. They'll take him in until I can talk to Barnabas." Brody hesitated. "What are your feelings about him?"

"I think he was telling the truth. We'll need to look into that envelope. Or have you already?"

Brody shook his head. "Not yet. Not without you. We'll look at it at home." He glanced at his watch. "I have to meet Brendon in an hour or so. We need to get moving."

"Sure. Whatever." Ker was still thinking about the man who had approached them, a frown across her face again. "How did he find us?"

"That I asked him. He said he had been wandering around the area, recognized you, and took a chance on approaching us. Don't worry. I won't let him near you until we get this resolved."

"Thank you, sweetheart." Her hand in his as they walked towards his truck, Ker's steps slowed. "Brody? What's on your truck?"

"I have no idea. I don't like it. Back to the diner, Kitten. Paul was just coming in off duty. I'll catch him to take a look."

They stood just inside the diner, watching closely as Paul approached the building. He had a grim look on his face. As he entered, he pointed towards the hallway that led to Lee's office.

"Paul? I don't like that look." Brody spoke as soon as Paul closed the door behind him.

"I've called in the bomb squad, Brody. I'm not taking any chances. We've heard what's been going on." Paul peeked around the door as a tap came and he spoke quietly to whoever it was. "I'll be back. I want you two to stay in here. If you're expected anywhere, call or text them that you're delayed. Just not why. Not until we can sort it out." He was gone, the door shut behind him before either of the couple could speak.

Brody sent off a quick text to Brendon, not really aware of what he was saying, and not knowing the consternation and fear that text would cause. He paced the office, Ker watching him from where she had perched on the corner of the desk.

Dallas peeked around the door before he entered, his eyes on the two in front of him. He shook his head. Lord, when can this be over? This is getting worse and worse for these two. I hate to be the ones to tell them this.

"Dallas? You're here?" Ker tilted her head to watch him.

"I am. Ker. Brody. Walk me through the last twenty-four hours." Dallas notepad and pen were out as he sat behind the desk.

Brody did just that, leaving out the part about the envelope. He wasn't ready to share that with Dallas, not yet. Ker watched him, shaking her head at him. Dallas watched the silent communication between the two.

"What did he leave you? And don't tell me that he didn't."

Brody sighed, holding up the envelope. "This. We haven't had a chance to look at it yet."

"May I?" Dallas' voice was stern as he asked.

"Only if you do it in front of us and let us see what is in it. Otherwise, it was given to us and is private material." Ker was digging in her heels, wanting it to be all over, but not willing to give up control of something this small.

"Okay, Ker. We can do that." Dallas reached into his pocket for latex gloves, snapped them on, and then opened the envelope, pulling out the documents.

Brody and Ker crowded close, watching and reaching each one.

"This doesn't make sense, Dallas." Ker was puzzled. "I don't know these people. Who are they?"

"That's what we need to find out. Are you sure he was legit?"

———

Brody shrugged. "He seemed that way. We spent hours talking and praying. The thing of it is? When Ker went over the paperwork with our lawyers, there was a power of attorney in his name. He says it was forged."

"Okay. I'll talk to John, was it?" At Brody's nod, Dallas tucked away his notepad and pen. "I'll leave this with you. If you can make copies for me, I would appreciate it."

"We will, at some point." Brody looked towards the door, fatigue weighing him down. "What about my truck?"

"Your truck? Oh, that. It was a bomb, Dallas. Set as a threat more than likely. Who did you anger?"

"Me? I have no idea. Unless it's whoever Kelly was working with."

"That's what we think. It will be a while yet before you can have your truck. If you're wanting to leave, I'll make sure that you have a ride home." Dallas looked around as he heard footsteps stop behind him. "Abe?"

"Dallas. Brody. Ker. We've been looking for you two. Brendon was worried." Abe's voice gave nothing away, nor did his face.

"I know. I was to meet with him." Brody looked down at Ker. "Any chance of a ride?"

"Sure. We'll take you home."

"We?" Brody peered at him. "Just how many are we?"

"All of us. Emma sent us."

"Emma? That's bad." Brody reached for Ker's hand. "Back door?"

"Of course. We're parked right outside. We have two vehicles, Brody. One of you in each."

"No way. I'm not leaving Brody." Ker's anger flared briefly.

"Ker, let them do it their way. This is how they work. This is how they keep people alive." Brody watched her until she gave a reluctant nod. "Who's Ker with?"

"You're with Joseph, Ian, Micah, and Luke. Ker is with Nathaniel, Murphy, Matt, and me." Abe quickly moved them to the vehicles and watched behind him as they drove away, heading for the Foundation building before the SUV in front of him pulled to the side, Murphy who was driving theirs following suit.

Abe was out of his vehicle, Micah coming towards him.

"Micah?"

"Emma called. She was trying to reach you but couldn't. There's news." Micah looked up, trying to find words. "It's Keefe."

"No. Not Keefe." Abe grew stern. "What happened?"

"He's admitted that he knew what his mother had been up to the last few months. He was trying to get away, to find someone who could help. That's when his father sent him away."

"This is not going to help Ker. Not a bit. She's sure, I know." Abe turned to stare at the vehicle behind him. "We need to take them home. It's almost to the point where we would normally hide our friends."

"I know. That won't work with this couple. Brody is ready to break free and go after them himself."

"I know, and we can't let them." Abe rubbed at his chin. "We take them home and make sure that they stay put."

"It won't work, Abe. Not there. What was going on at the restaurant?"

"A bomb on his truck. I sent Barnabas a text that we had them and were heading their way." Abe finally turned. "Head on out, Micah."

Abe slid back into his seat, nodding at Murphy. He turned slightly to watch Ker, finding her eyes on him.

"What happened, Abe?"

"We need to talk, Ker, but I want Brody there."

She paled. "Keefe?"

"He's okay, Ker. We'll connect you two today."

"Do more than connect. I need my brother and I need him now. Please?" Ker knew she was begging but she just needed her older brother.

"We'll see what we can do. Right now, we need to get you two back home." Abe shifted around to watch the area around them. "Someone's out there, fellows."

———

"I know." Matt had been watching the area. "And there's a truck behind it. It pulled over when we did."

"Can you get the plate number?" Abe ducked his head to stare out the back window.

"No. He's staying back far enough that we can't." Matt was frustrated.

Chapter 39

Barnabas approached Abe, watching as Brody and Ker were hustled quickly into the building, Abe's men surrounding them, his own men watching from the sidelines.

"Abe? Where did you find them?"

"At a diner called Lee's. They had been there all night, from what I was told. They met someone named Lowe."

"Lowe? That name came up in our research. But all night?" Barnabas was puzzled.

"Lowe. Ker said that they made sure he had something to eat, Brody sent him to the shelter, and then when they went to leave, a bomb was found on Brody's truck."

"A bomb?" Breck let out a whistle. "Someone means business."

"They do. We need to talk, Barnabas. This is getting out of hand. We can't lock them up, but we need to work with you and your security and the local police to determine just what we do."

"Brody won't do that." Breck was adamant in his statement. "And Ker is getting angry. It has been building for years, I would say. She's just as apt to go after whoever it is."

"Don't let her. If you have to, stage the confrontation where you can control it. And there will be a confrontation, that much I can guarantee." Abe watched as his team returned, mingling among the building men for a while before heading for the vehicles. "We need to get on the road. We're leaving tonight for a week. Call Emma if you need to reach me."

"We will." Barnabas shook Abe's hand and then stood back.

The two men watched the vehicles leave before they turned to find all twelve of the Foundation men behind them. They could see the ladies in the lobby, watching as well.

"Brody? What didn't you tell Abe?" Breck walked towards him.

"This." Brody held up the envelope. "Dallas has looked through it. Lowe gave it to us. We need to talk about what he said." Fatigue was making it difficult for him to talk.

"You need to catch some sleep first, Brody." Brendon reached for the envelope. "Head off and get some. We'll meet later this afternoon. You know where to find us."

They watched as Brody hesitated, nodded, and walked away, his arm coming out to gather Ker to him.

"He's about at the end of what he can take. He hasn't let himself heal." Brady spoke as he followed their progress.

"No, he hasn't. And he won't, not until it's all over."

"And that will keep Ker from relaxing as well." Buckley shook his head. "This is the part, isn't it, fellows, where we need to pray and pray hard."

"It is, Buckley. Prayer chain at work?" Bradon grinned at his friend even as he headed for the conference room.

"Absolutely. I didn't have to start it this time. Your wife took care of that. I'm putting her in charge."

"Really? She'll enjoy that." Bradon stood in front of the map. "So, where do we go from here? It's centred back around our town once more."

"It always comes back to that, doesn't it?" Burnie stood beside him, a frown on his face. "I always have felt that there was a common theme running through all the adventures. That there's someone else involved that we have not figured out yet."

"That's what we all think. But going back to Lowe, what's in the envelope?" Brendon walked over to where Breck had opened it and laid out the paperwork.

"We need to find out what their discussion was. But this is interesting. Proof of a stolen identity. Police statements. Copies of his identity. And a letter was written to Ker and Keefe from him." Breck sorted through it. "I think it will help move us forward. He names people. Anyone recognize them?" He passed around that piece of paper.

Brandon took it, heading to make copies of it. "We'll each need a copy. A copy of everything and then the originals get sealed into an envelope. He said Dallas has seen it?"

"He did. That helps." Blair took the papers as they were copied, sorting them out and then handing them around.

Four hours later, Brody stood in the doorway, Ker beside him, watching as the men worked away. He had spoken with Dallas, who had confirmed that the bomb had been meant for him. There had been a note inside it. Whoever it was had seemed to think that Brody would not open the box himself.

"Brody? Where do we go from here? They want to lock us up somewhere. I couldn't stand that." Ker drew closer to Brody, leaning against him.

"Nor could I. But if it becomes necessary, we'll have to." Brody nodded towards the men. "They've been at work while I've been sleeping. So have you."

Ker looked down at the sheaf of papers she held. "I was. But I don't know that I did any good. What I found from newspaper articles doesn't make a lot of sense."

"It might when we put it all together." Brody walked them over to the table he favoured and seated her.

Baird approached. "Brody? You two are okay?"

"We are, so far. Thanks for asking. Where do we stand?"

———

"Further ahead but still not there." Baird blew out a breath of frustration. "We're missing something, Brody, Ker. Just what it is, we're not sure of."

"Can we somehow visualize what you have found out? Sometimes, that makes it easier." Ker looked at the wall. "And I can see that you've started that."

"We have. It's a continuation of the logic puzzle. That we've been able to sort out more for."

Chapter 40

A week later, Ker approached Brody as he stood on the balcony in the early morning sunlight, his hands clasping the railing. He simply reached to pull her close to him, loving her more each day. He reached to kiss her, finding her face upturned for that.

"Ker? Have I told you today that I love you?"

She smiled, content to be held. "You have. I love you, too." She seemed unsettled for a moment. "Brody? Someone has found my new phone number. There were a lot of awful brutal texts sent overnight."

Brody stared down at the phone that she was thrusting at him. "They have? You read them?"

"I started to and then stopped. I don't want a phone. Not if this is what is happening."

"We'll get you another one." Brody turned them back into the apartment. "Let me call Dallas."

"I did already. He's not in today. I turned the phone off. I don't want them sending anymore." She paced the office, not looking at him, her arms wrapped around herself.

Brody watched her closely, seeing how fragile that she had become in the last couple of weeks. "I wish that I could just take you away somewhere and come back when this is all over."

"I wish you could. I pray every night that I will wake up and find this over or at least that it's a bad dream. That never happens. What am I supposed to be learning through all this, Brody?"

"That I don't know. To trust more, I guess. To seek God in a deeper way." He stared down at her phone. "Let's tuck this away. Dallas is in tomorrow?"

"They said that he would be. They promised to give him my message." Ker was hesitant in how she spoke. "This is so different from what I am used to."

"I am sure it is. We have a good force here." Brody glanced at the clock. "It's too early to go downstairs."

"And why? Does the door not open until a certain time?" Ker was challenging him, she knew.

He shot her a look and then began to laugh. "You have me there. No, it doesn't. We have spent all-nighters in there at times." He reached for her hand. "Let's head down there, then."

His phone ringing as they walked towards the room had him reaching for it, a frown on his face.

"It's Abe. I thought they were to be away."

"I thought so, too. Answer it."

Brody listened as Abe spoke quickly, asking only the question "When" before he pocketed his phone and reached to wrap Ker into a hug.

"Brody?" When he didn't respond, she pushed at him. "Brody? What did Abe want?"

"He and Emma are heading this way. This morning. And Keefe is coming." He watched as her eyes sank closed before they popped open again.

"Keefe? Is it safe?"

"They seem to think so. Emma has more information for us. He said it would be a flying visit, but Keefe would be staying if we can arrange that."

"And of course, we can. Can't we?"

"That we can." Brody studied her again. "Are you ready for this?"

"I think so. I mean, we need to talk. Doing that over the phone doesn't work so well." Ker pulled the door open and looked in. "I thought that you said it was too early. It doesn't look that way."

Brody laughed. "No, it doesn't." A hand to her back, he directed her in, heading for Breck. "Here. Ker's been getting a lot of messages on her phone."

"She has? We wondered. And it's a number that shouldn't be out there."

"No, it's not. Dallas is out of the office today, so we'll turn it in tomorrow. If you need to take a look at it, here's the password." Brody scrawled it down for him.

"Thanks, Brody." Breck peered at Ker, watching as she wandered around, reading the papers on the wall. "How is she?"

"Hurting in many ways, Breck. Abe and Emma are heading this way today. Keefe is with them. Abe said that he'd talk to you about what to do for security for him."

"It may make it easier having them together, but it may make it harder." Breck rose, setting the phone on the desk. "Let me go talk with security. See what we need to do."

"Thanks, Breck." Brody stood, lost in thought before a hand on his shoulder roused him from his thoughts, some of which were dark.

"Brody?" Blair stood there, his eyes shifting between Brody and Ker. "How are you both?"

"That is a question that I really don't know how to answer. Ker is hurting in ways that I can't make better for her. Keefe is heading this way today."

"He is? That's good, isn't it?" Blair was unsure of how to read Brody about this.

"It is, and then again, it might not be." Brody blew out a breath. "I'm really not sure how to take it. Ker wants to see him, but she is afraid."

"Afraid of what she might find out from him? Or afraid that he'll be hurt if he's around her?"

"Both, I think. I know that I have real hesitations about him coming. What if he has been involved all along?"

"I talked to Abe earlier. A friend met with him. She's a retired forensics psychologist. She didn't pick up that he was the culprit or that Ker needs to fear him. And Abe said she is one of the best he has ever seen at reading people without meeting them in person. She's even better when she can sit down with the person."

"That's good to know." Brody looked around. "You fellows have been busy in here all night, haven't you? Where do we stand?"

"That's what we need to discuss." Benen had moved closer. "We have some research that we need to clarify with Ker. Brody, in your job, did you ever come across someone who tried to bribe you?"

Brody's eyes shot to him, shock on his face. "I did. About a year ago. I had forgotten. I never got the woman's name or any more details from her. Once she tried to offer me a bribe, I cut the conversation off. I don't even know if I have the number for her now."

"Then, that's part of how you got involved." Benen held out a file folder. "Read this. You'll need to talk to Ker as well."

Chapter 41

Looking up from where she had been reading, Ker frowned. The men were quiet, which she found unusual. They were usually joking with one another. Right now, they were all deep in concentration, the occasional question or comment from one to the other breaking the silence. She rose, wandering around the room, needing to move but not wanting to leave where Brody was.

Brody watched her closely, noting the distress on her face before he looked back down at his notes. He sighed, threw down his pen, and rose, heading for his bride.

"Kitten? How be we take a walk around the lobby? We both need a break from here."

"Sure." She shrugged as she took the hand that he held out for her. "Did Abe say when they would arrive?"

"No, he didn't. Just sometime this morning." Brody paced with her, his hand holding hers tight. "When this is over, do you want to run away with me for a few days?"

"You would do that?" She looked up at him. "Where?"

He shrugged. "We could find a nice hotel. Or a cabin in the woods. Or go camping."

"I've never been to a cabin in the woods or camping. Can I think about it?"

"I guess. I was hoping to know today." He laughed at her look of outrage. "It's okay, Kitten. You can think about it, and we'll make the decision together." He smiled widely. "I like the sounds of that. Making decisions together."

"You do, huh? And if we don't agree?" She smirked at his own pretended look of outrage.

"Then, we compromise. We go where you want and then next time where I want."

"Sounds like a plan." Ker's footsteps slowed as she stared through the window, her attention on the vehicle stopped just outside the door. "Keefe?"

"It's Abe and Emma. And that is your brother?"

"It is. It's Keefe. What happened to him? He looks sick."

"He has been, Kitten. Abe hasn't told us where they found him or what happened to him. That, I think, was likely for your own protection."

Keefe Deeks stared up at the building, amazement on his face. "This is the Foundation building?"

"It is, Keefe. The main offices are here. Each of the men who live here has an apartment and also an office. There are a physician and his wife on site as well." Abe watched him closely, knowing how close it had been to losing him as well. "Brody and Ker are here. Just inside the building doors."

"They are." Keefe's attention went to the door. "Can I go in?"

"You can. In fact, it's likely best that we get you inside and under cover." Abe's hand gripped Keefe's elbow to steady him, Emma on his other side with his bag in her hand.

Keefe stopped just inside the door, looking around, his attention drawn to the comfortable feeling of the lobby before he caught movement in front of him. He frowned for a moment and then his face cleared.

"Ker? You're here?"

"Keefe!" Ker broke from Brody and ran for her brother, finding his arms open to receive her hug, Abe's hand on his back to steady him.

Ker's sobs shook Brody as he heard them from where he had moved closer. He finally just reached to encircle the siblings with his arms, his quiet prayer reaching them and calming Ker. She looked up at him, mouthing a thank you to him before she studied her brother.

"Brody, we need to get Keefe somewhere he can sit down."

"That we do. Abe, Emma? Are you with us or with the fellows in the conference room?"

"I'm with them. Abe's with you." Emma moved away rapidly, her worn sneaker scuffing softly across the floor.

"Abe?" Brody turned to him.

"Let's get him up to your place for now. I think your Doc will need to see him."

"We can do that. He's at work today." Brody reached for Ker's hand, watching her closely before he led the way to the elevator and then to their apartment.

Keefe sank gratefully down onto the couch, his hand held tight in Ker's. He was exhausted but glad to be with his remaining family. They needed to talk, he knew, but it would come.

"Ker? You're okay? You're happy?" Keefe's eyes opened to watch her.

"I am, Keefe. This is not how I expected to be married. In fact, I didn't think I ever would. Brody is the one God meant for me. That much I know." Ker watched him. "And now you're here. Keefe, are you really okay?"

"I'm getting there, sis. It will be a while. Whatever they gave me drained me and kept me in a stupor of some kind. I just don't know what it was. Abe here said I was on my own when they found me. I don't remember much, other than Dad insisting that I take my vacation at that time."

"I wondered about that. He also arranged for Brody to come in to go over legal documents. That I found it strange that he didn't meet with him. He was afraid for us."

"I think so. I would find him up late at night, working away in his home office. When I would ask him what I could to help, he just waved me away. I did find information that he was planning on shutting down the agency.”

“He was? I wondered. Just something that I felt. Did they tell you how he went?”

Keefe nodded. “His heart. He denied that he had any problems, but I could see his health was failing.” He sighed, his eyes closing. “I’m sorry about Mom, Ker.”

“Why?” Ker shared a look with Brody, who had sat on the arm of the couch, his arm around her, and with Abe, who had seated himself across from them.

“Because you deserved to have a different mother. One who you could have pleased, been friends with. And that you didn’t have. You don’t know the number of times that I stepped in to shield you.”

Ker reached to hug her brother, tears sparkling on her eyelashes. “I know, Keefe. I know of some of them. Mom made sure that I did.”

Chapter 42

Breck paused in the hallway of Brody's apartment, his eyes on Keefe as he slept, before he moved to the kitchen, thanking Brody for the mug of coffee handed to him. He sat, his eyes on Ker, as she too slept, her head pillowed on her arms, a blanket wrapped around her.

"She okay?"

"She will be. She's taken it well, but it bothers her how Keefe was treated. She wants the culprits for that."

"We're tracking them. I spoke with Dallas earlier. He was around, just to take Ker's phone. He's talked to Will, and both feel that they need to work on that. Dallas did say that they were closing in on some of the lower echelons, as he put it."

"That's good, as long as it doesn't cause the head ones to run." Brody sat beside her, his arm around her. "She can't take much more. She's struggling in her faith, the longer this goes on."

"I know that she is. So are you. Do you need to talk, Brody?"

"Not at present, but at some point, I likely will." Brody paused. "What have you discovered about the documents that Lowe gave us?"

"They are legit. That much we know. Dallas didn't say much about them, just took the copies we gave him. He's wearing out, Brody."

"That he is. We've done that to him."

"No, I don't think so. I mean, maybe to some degree, but there's more. His interests are changing, I think. He's not sure what he wants, is what I'm picking up."

"I get that feeling too." Brody sighed again, his eyes on Ker's face. "I want this over, Breck. How do we do that?"

"We'll take to Keefe. Put together what he can remember with what Ker has. Match it to what we have found out. Our concern is that we won't find out who it is in time, and Ker or you disappear."

"I know. That worries me. It is keeping me up at night, trying to think about how to keep her safe. I have to be back in the office next week. I have no choice. There are some cases and documents that I need to deal with."

"We get that, Brody. The security head has been working on that. They'll take you in and bring you home. If Ker has to go with you, your employer has said that's okay. We've tried to think of everything that we could to try and keep you two safe."

"We appreciate it." Brody was silent for a moment. "Breck, can I run something by you? Something that has puzzled me all along."

"Sure." Breck reached for the pad of paper and pen lying beside him. "I see that you were prepared."

Brody grinned. "Always." He sobered. "Okay, say Keefe was not taken to keep him quiet. That's what we assumed. What if he was taken as a threat against Keane? Or against Ker?" He paused. "But, what if there is another party involved? Keefe was taken as a threat to Kelly? To make her cooperate with them? Only she refused to? That's why Keefe was kept as he was?"

"That's an interesting supposition, Brody. Bradon mentioned that this morning. He seems to think that might be the case. He's working on that, trying to find whatever information that he can."

"And what about you? What are your feelings?" Brody watched Breck closely.

"I think that there is merit in that." Breck looked around to find Keefe standing beside him. "Hi. I'm Breck."

"What you said? How serious were you?" Keefe pulled out a chair, slumping down in it.

"Serious enough that two of our men are heading up that way today. Our Foundation pilot is flying them up." Breck watched Keefe closely.

"Good. My mind has been so foggy but it's starting to clear. I can remember Dad asking me to take my holidays at that time, even though I didn't really want to. He was insistent that I did. For some reason. He never said, but he had been distracted lately."

"What can you remember about that?"

"Not a lot. He wouldn't say much. Not unless he had proof. And if he had proof, then he would confront that person." He groaned. "I can remember him and Mom arguing that last day before I left. He was calm but stern. She was excited, angry, loud. She wasn't like that." Keefe studied his still-sleeping sister. "I can remember Ker being mentioned. I couldn't hear what Mom said, but I heard Dad tell her that there was no way Ker was going somewhere. I left the next day."

"And where did you end up?"

"I headed towards Toronto but never made it. Someone ran me off the road, shoved me into another vehicle, and tied me up. I could see my car following us. Then, we traveled for hours, ending up near the Quebec border. I was shoved into a room with no windows, the door locked. They must have drugged me at that point. I don't remember much until Abe had me at his place. And I can't describe the men. They seemed to be disguised."

Chapter 43

Late that night, Brody stared at his computer screen, reading an email that had reached him through his work account. He paled, re-reading it, before he was on his feet, moving rapidly through the apartment, searching it. He pulled out microphones from the office and the living room. His face grew stern. Someone had been in his apartment. The only ones, beside Breck and themselves, were the cleaners.

He stood for the longest time, watching Ker sleep, before he turned away, looking for his phone, sending off a text message to all the fellows. Responses were quick, and he heard a tapping at his door.

Breck and Brandon stood there, Brendon and Blair coming up behind them. Brody stood back and pointed to the kitchen.

"I have coffee on. We're going to need it." He handed out the mugs of coffee and then the email that he had printed. "This is what came through my work email. They have been in our apartment."

"So they have. What did you find?" Brandon looked up.

"Microphones in the office and living room. Nowhere else. No cameras." Brody pointed to the counter. "There they are. I'll contact Dallas in the morning. This has gone too far, fellows. I want to go on the offensive. Put out a statement or two."

"We can do that." Breck nodded. "We'll work with the lawyers and the police public relations."

"No, not the police. On our own. We'll let them know what we plan, but this is for us, Breck. For Ker and myself. For Keefe. They won't stop coming after them until we do. They're cowards and bullies."

"They are. Before we do anything though, we pray. We don't go out there until and unless God says that we do." Breck watched with compassion as Brody finally nodded. "I know that it's tough, Brody, but we can't move without God being there."

"I know, Breck. I get that. I just want this over. Can we do that?"

"We can." Brandon looked up at him. "I found some new information just a bit ago. I have verified it but haven't had a chance to talk to anyone else."

"And that would be?" Brody wanted answers.

"That Kelly had a brother who ran with a shady group. She kept in touch with him behind Keane's back. He is the one who was behind what happened to Keefe. The police in that area arrested the men and they talked. Emma was able to get that information for us. They have a warrant out for his arrest. The thing of it is, he's in this area."

"Lowe?"

"That's who we suspect. You wouldn't have known when you met with him. Dallas was in touch late this afternoon. The documents are all forgeries."

"And he seemed so earnest and honest. Ker had sensed a hesitation about him. We talked through the night. He gives a good line."

"That's what the men who were arrested have said. They said that he was out for revenge, but would play it like he was the one hard done by."

"And that's exactly how he played it." Brody watched Ker as she moved slightly before he rose, scooped her into his arms, and headed for the bedroom, to tuck her into bed. He stood for a moment, praying for her, knowing that they were heading into the roughest part of what they faced.

"Breck, now what?" Brody reached for his mug, refreshing his coffee before he sat again.

"We keep you two as safe as we can. We work on your publicity request. If the lawyers say no, Brody, we don't go ahead with it. We have to weigh your safety against what we could find out by doing that. How prepared are you for further violence against you or Ker?"

"I'm not, but I know that we could face it anywhere or at any time. As I said, I want this over with and soon."

The men bent their heads and discussed the options, finally coming up with a plan.

"You'll talk to Ker, I take it, Brody?" Brendon looked up finally.

"I will. We need to do this, fellows. They're hiding. And when they're hiding, they'll strike at us when we least expect it. I don't want that."

"We understand, Brody." Breck paused before he spoke again. "Let's pray, okay? We need that."

Chapter 44

Ker shifted uneasily late the next morning. She had not seen Keefe, for some reason, and she was glad that she had not. Something was off about him, and she just could not place what it was. He wasn't the brother that she remembered. She ran quickly down the stairs and headed for the conference room, needing the company that she was sure that she would find there. And she was right. Most of the fellows and all of the ladies were gathered there, looking up as she shut the door carefully behind her.

Fynn approached her, a frown on her face. "Ker? What is going on? You are white!"

"I am? Oh, no. That's not good. I just thought of something and needed to talk to someone."

"Well, I'm here. So are the other ladies. What can we do for you? Here, come over to this corner. We staked our claim on it."

"Staked a claim?" Ennis began to laugh as she heard Fynn. "Fynn, your language and description at times leaves a lot to be desired."

"Well, it's exactly what we did. Isn't it? Ker, sit. And no, I don't think that you're a dog."

The ladies broke out into merry laughter, Ker staring at Fynn for a moment.

"Fynn, stop while you're ahead. You're just making it worse." Cadee grinned at Ker. "Now, that you're here, we're all set. First, let's get you your tea." She was up and away, back quickly with the tea that she knew Ker preferred.

"You're spoiling me, ladies." Ker smiled at them.

"And you deserve to be. We've been where you are right now." Berneen looked up again from her paperwork. "Now, Ker, what can we do for you? You're troubled."

"I am. You know that Keefe has arrived."

"We do. How is he?" Devaney looked Ker over carefully.

"I really don't know. He sounds like my brother and looks like him, but there is something off. Something he has said that just doesn't ring true to what I know." Ker was troubled by what she had remembered Keefe saying.

"And what would that be?" Guenivere had her pen ready to write. "Or can you share it?"

"I can. I need to go back a bit. Keefe has always tied to defend me and protect me, sometimes to my distress and against my wishes. He said that he heard Mom and Dad fighting but couldn't understand what they were fighting about. He also said he approached Dad late one night. He couldn't have. He had his own place and spent little time at home. He was never there late at night."

"That is concerning, Ker. What else?" Hagen looked around at the ladies even as Imly made notes.

"There is just something off about how he is talking. He doesn't sound or talk like Keefe would."

"Was he drugged?" Fynn watched as Ker nodded. "Sometimes drugs do that, but not to the extent of what you're saying. There's more?"

"There is. Someone was sending me texts and voice mail to the new phone that Brody got me. Keefe was the only one other than Abe, Emma, and all of you who had that number. Was it him or did someone get it from him?"

"I would suggest that we need to talk to whoever it was that he was staying with at Abe's." Devaney sent off a quick message. "Emma will get back to us as soon as she can."

"But who would do this?" Ker was troubled and it showed.

"Whoever it is that is behind all this. This Lowe fellow? Do you trust him?" Imly looked up once more.

"Not really. I slept unfortunately most of the time we were together. Brody talked to him at length, but I don't know that he trusted him fully. Cadee, he sent him to the shelter."

"He did. Dad has talked to him. He's not sure that he's on the level, as he put it." Cadee smiled sadly. "Dad has a good read on people."

"He does." Ennis looked around, seeing Brady watching them closely. "Brady's watching us."

"He is?" Ker turned slightly. "Brody's not here. I thought that he was."

"Breck and Barnabas have him in the Foundation office. Something about legal paperwork that they wanted him to go over with the lawyers." Imly looked around. "It's lunchtime, ladies. Let's put out the sandwiches and whatever it is that we brought, eat, spend some time in prayer and then reconvene."

Chapter 45

Looking behind him, Breck sighed. So much for having security with him. They had been separated from Brody and himself. The three men behind him were not them. Barnabas had sent Breck and Brody into the courthouse with documents that needed to be filed. They all thought that they had taken the precautions that they needed. Obviously not.

"Breck? What happened to the security?" Brody looked around. "I don't see them."

"They're not with us. Somehow, they were separated from us in this crowd. We have a tail of three men that we need to lose." Breck made a sudden move, pulling a door open and tugging Brody with him. "Down this way. This leads to the basement and then out to the parking lot. There's a path that we can take to get to the street. Not many people know of it."

"I certainly didn't. How did you?"

"Growing up here as a kid, you explored. This is one that we explored often. We used to be able to wander the courthouse, but it's too locked down now." Breck shoved open a door, squinting against the sudden light. "Wait for a moment."

Brody waited, barely daring to breathe, shooting quick glances over his shoulder.

"Breck?" He kept his voice low.

"It looks okay, but I'm not sure." He let the door close, glancing around. "There, that hallway. It will take us back upstairs, to the outside door." He ran quickly, Brody on his heels.

The men popped outside, searching for the men who had been following them, not seeing them. They ran for the parking lot, finding the security team frantically searching for them.

"Breck! Brody! What happened to you two?" The older of the three men hustled them into the truck.

"We were separated from you and followed. I found the old tunnels under the courthouse."

"Good thinking. We saw the men. Dallas was here for a court case. He stopped them and they took them in. We were trying to find you." The man stared at them. "What else?"

Brody shook his head. "Nothing. Just that someone seems to be keeping a fairly close eye on us."

"Someone has been. They've been around the perimeter again, Breck. We'll up the security there for now."

"I know you will. It's what they always do, try and catch our people out in the open. Only Brody and Ker haven't been playing that game."

"Not yet. But it's coming. We need to go on the offensive, Breck. Ker is ready to snap." Brody was growing angry. "I know God is in all this, but it seems as if He's gone quiet."

"It always seems that way, Brody. You know that from the others. Let's meet again with the fellows and see what we can come up with."

Breck and Brody stood in the conference room thirty minutes later, staring around, not seeing anyone.

"They should be here." Breck paced the room. "They were planning on working all day."

"I know. No word from anyone?" Brody walked closer to the tables. "Wait. Their phones. They are all on the tables. What is going on?" He spun as the door opened.

"We've been waiting for you two." Lowe stood there, sneering at them. "Fooled you, didn't I?"

"No, not really." Brody stood, arms crossed. "Not really. You put on a good show. You should be in the movies. I thought back over what we had talked about. You just didn't ring true with some of your words."

"Is that right? Well, let's see how these words ring true. We have your friends and the ladies. They are separated into two different rooms. No one gets hurt if you come with us."

Brody snorted, causing Breck to stare at him. "No? I would suspect that you've already roughed up some of them. It's what you do. I spoke with Dallas this morning. He warned me that you were not who you said. So, who is Lowe?"

"Lowe? What makes you think I'm not him?"

"Fingerprints, for one. DNA. You shouldn't have eaten in the diner. Not when the two brothers of the owner are patrol officers. You threw out garbage that they confiscated and took in for testing. It proves that you're not Lowe. In fact, you're Kelly Deeks' cousin. You're the one who kidnapped Keefe. Threatened my wife. Who is behind you?"

"No one. I'm the boss."

Brody shook his head. "No, you're not. You're not that smart. You left a few clues in the bomb that you deposited on my truck. That note? It wasn't written by you. It's too sophisticated to have been."

"You think you're that smart?" Lowe raised his arm, bringing his weapon down on Brody's head before either he or Breck could react. Brody dropped to the floor, his eyes closed. "Pick him up. I said, pick him up."

Breck did that, carefully dropping Brody over his shoulder, his eyes on Lowe.

"Now what?"

"Now what, is that you follow me. We'll find the ladies. The men will cooperate if the ladies are threatened. It always works."

Breck gave a grim smile. "And you think the ladies will just do what you want?"

"Of course they will. They're too chicken to do anything else."

Breck simply shook his head, walking towards the outside door and then towards the gym near the other side of the parking lot. "You put the woman in the gym?"

"Sure. Why not?" Lowe stared at him before he shook his head. "They won't try anything."

Breck snorted and then corrected himself with only a gleam of satisfaction in his eyes. He knew the ladies. They would find weapons of some kind in there. They would not let these men win.

Lowe pulled open the door, waiting until Breck had entered and deposited Brody gently to the floor before he too entered and looked around.

"What on..?" Lowe spun, staring around the room, seeing the men that he had left with the women unconscious on the floor. "Where are they?"

"I have no idea, but I can guarantee you that they'll find the men, release them, and then come back for you." Breck leaned against the wall, his arms folded across his chest. "Did you really think that the women who had gone through life and death struggles would sit still for you to destroy them and the fellows?"

"And why wouldn't they?"

"Because they are survivors. They are fighters. They don't take what you dish out sitting down." Breck paused, his gaze on the ceiling before he smiled and looked back at Lowe. "Because God is in control." He moved quickly to one side, ducking as a body flew through the air, a wild cry sounding, and feet slammed into Lowe, sending him unconscious to the floor.

Fynn stood up, dusting off her hands, as the other ladies ran from the locker areas.

"Fynn? You could have been hurt! But thank you!" Ker reached to hug her friend. She poked at Lowe with her toe before she dropped beside Brody. "What did he do?"

"Knocked him out. He'll be around soon." Breck stood back up from where he had been bent over tying up Lowe. "You've tied up the others?"

"We have. Now, we need to find our fellows." Ennis was angry and ready to fight.

"This is how we do it. We move Brody back into the security office. Some of you ladies will stay with him. Some of you will come with me. Figure it out among yourselves. Now, move." Breck had Brody over his shoulder again and moving quickly for the main building.

Chapter 46

Raising a finger, Breck pointed to the office, heading that way and gently laying Brody down. Ker was beside him, his head on her lap, her hands feeling his head.

"He's got a bad lump here." She looked up to find Cadee beside her, an ice pack in her hand. "Thank you. Breck? Who stays and who goes?"

"You and Cadee stay here. Cadee has medical training. Now, ladies?" Breck looked around with a grin at the angry looks on their faces. "Who goes and who stays?"

"Imly stays. Hagen?"

"We'll stay. The rest of you go find our fellows. We want this over today. It's gone on long enough. Now that they have threatened all of us, we will work together to end it." Hagen followed them to the door, shutting it and locking it. Imly reached for a chair, to brace it under the knob.

"That should hold out anyone. Our guys will batter at the door, I know." Hagen looked around, reaching for the phone. "It's dead. They've cut our communications."

"Here. Brody still has his. I can call for help." Ker dialed Dallas, finding him in the office. "Dallas? We need help."

"Ker?" Dallas sounded distracted. "Where are you?"

"At the moment? Imly, Hagen, Cadee, and I are locked into the security office with an unconscious Brody. Breck and the other ladies are searching for the fellows who are locked up somewhere. Lowe and some of his cronies are tied up in the gym. The phone system is down."

"Ker? What are you talking about? I just called and spoke with Barnabas." Dallas' voice died away. "But come to think of it, he didn't sound like he normally does. How many?"

"How many what? Minutes? Hours? Men?"

"Ker! How many men?"

"About eight and Lowe. There are three plus Lowe tied up. He didn't think that he needed to leave more than that with us."

"Obviously he was wrong." Dallas strode rapidly through the department, looking for Will. "Ker, I'm going to hang up. We're on our way."

Ker stared at the phone. "He hung up on me!"

"Of course he did. It's what they always do, isn't it?" Hagen looked around. "Now, we need to find something that we can defend ourselves with if we need to." She looked around as Brody's phone rang. "You need to mute that."

"I know." Ker stared at the number. "Abe? Why are you calling?"

"Ker? Where are you?" Abe's voice echoed over the phone.

"Locked in the security room. Why?"

"Because we got word that Lowe was going to try something today."

Ker laughed. "Well, guess what! You're too late with the warning. He already did. Fynn took him out. Oh, what a sight that was!"

"Ker? What are you talking about?"

"They separated us, ladies and fellows. We managed to take out the men watching us as they say. Then, we hid. Lowe showed up with Brody and Breck. Fynn flew down from the rafters on a rope, knocking Lowe out. And Brody is hurt."

"Where are the fellows?" Ker could hear Abe speaking with someone.

"That we don't know. Breck and the ladies are searching for them. It's just Cadee, Hagen, Imly, and myself with Brody."

"Do you have help on the way?"

"We do. Dallas is coming. Why? Where are you?"

"Not where we can help, unfortunately. Emma just reached out to me. She couldn't raise any of you."

"Of course, she couldn't. They made us leave our phones in the conference room. Breck and Brody were off site when the men arrived. That's how I have Brody's phone. Brody! You need to lie still. Please!

Abe? I need to go." Ker hung up on Abe as he protested.

"Ker? You're okay? The others?" Brody tried to sit up and then slumped back down. "My head hurts."

"Of course it does. Lowe hit you over the head." Hagen knelt beside them. "We managed to take out his men in the gym and Lowe too."

Brody looked askance as the ladies laughed.

"We'll explain, sweetheart. Right now, let Cadee check your head."

"No cut but a bruise." Cadee slapped the ice pack back into his hand. "Keep this on it. It will help."

"I know it will but where are the others?"

"Breck and the other ladies are searching for the fellows. Dallas is on his way. And Abe called to warn us."

"Abe did? He's overseas." Brody studied Ker's face.

"I know. Emma couldn't reach us, so reached out to him. Yours is the only phone we have. They cut the lines or whatever it is that they do in the movies. There is no phone system."

Brody slumped back against Ker who simply wrapped her arms around her fellow, her chin on his shoulder. Hagen positioned herself near the door, listening for any sound from the hallway. Imly took up a position near the window, having closed the blinds, just keeping them open enough that she could watch the parking lot.

"Dallas is here." Her whisper sounded loud in the sudden silence. "Wow! He's got a lot of men and women with him."

"He thinks he needs them. This is a big place to search." Brody reached for his phone as it vibrated. "It's Dallas. He wants to know if we're still in the office."

Ker reached for the phone. "You're supposed to be unconscious. Let me answer him." Brody stared at her in disbelief, Imly and Hagen snickering.

Chapter 47

Sudden hammering at the door and jiggling of the doorknob startled them, causing squeaks to come from both Hagen and Imly. Hagen refused to move the chair or unlock the door, afraid that it was Lowe's men.

Brody looked up from his phone with a grin on his face.

"It's okay, Hagen. Breck and your fellows are outside. Dallas is with them." He kept grinning. "Go on. Open the door. They'll keep trying to break it down."

"I don't believe them. Have them send me a picture."

"A picture? Are you for real?" Brody was stunned at her response.

Ker simply took his phone, sent the text to Breck, and waited. A grin lit up her own face as she was on her feet, first showing the phone to Hagen and then to Imly.

"We can open the door. Hurry, Hagen." Imly was there beside her to help remove the chair.

The door was barely unlocked when it flew open and Brendon, Blair, and Brennen were through it, gathering their wives close to them. Breck moved towards Brody, a hand out to help him to his feet and then to steady him. Dallas stared among them all.

“You ladies are okay?”

Their chorus of “of course, we are” startled him before he too grinned.

“Good. Now, we need to have Brody here assessed and then we need to meet to talk.”

“I’m fine, Dallas. Just get this over with. Tell me one thing. Do you have the ringleader?”

“No, but we know who they are. Officers and detectives are heading that way now, with arrest warrants in hand.” Dallas turned and walked away, his voice trailing after him. “Conference room in ten.”

“Did he really say that?” Ker ran after him. “Dallas? Ten? Really?”

“Really, Ker. We need to get your statements while we can before you start talking with one another. You know that.”

“I do, but a little time would be nice. We’ll be there in thirty.” She spun and walked away, nose in the air, as he stared after her.

“I think that you were just told.” Buckley grinned at him. “I'll make sure that she’s there when you want her to be.”

“Do that.” Dallas’ words were clipped as he walked away. He hadn’t told them who the ringleaders were. They were people that not one of them had suspected.

Brody seated Ker in her favourite chair, moving to find tea for her. The other ladies had been in as had Anna and Doc, making sure the building inhabitants were all taken care of and unharmed. Doc had stopped him, checked his head, and then told him to come to see him the next morning. Ker took her tea, her hand reaching for Brody's as he sat beside her. She studied the room and then her friends, glad that it was over, she prayed, and that no one was harmed.

"Brody? Why?"

"That's what Dallas will tell us. He's still working through some of it. We've given our statements. Now, they have to take those, work through what we've said for charges against Lowe and his men. They also have to ensure that the cases are airtight for when they go to court. It takes time. He'll give us what he can tonight."

Dallas finally walked through the door, his mind and thoughts not on the men and ladies gathered there. He had had disturbing news from the arresting officers and sighed to himself. It was not what he had wanted to hear. He took the mug of coffee handed him with a quiet thanks before he found Barnabas.

"Barnabas? Can we spend some time in prayer? Your people need it and so do I."

"It's that bad?" Barnabas searched his friend's face.

"It is. I have no idea how Ker will take what I have to say." He searched the room. "Where's Keefe?"

"Doc has him. He collapsed during our adventure. He's in the infirmary. Two of your people are with him."

"Good. I'll talk to him later. How serious?"

"Doc didn't say. Let's get started on the prayers and then you can have the floor." Barnabas moved to the front of the room, drawing all eyes to himself as the room quieted. "Okay. Dallas is here and will speak in a bit. First, let's spend time in prayer. We all need it. Keep Keefe in your prayers are well."

Chapter 48

Dallas stood near the front of the room, his head bowed as he gathered his thoughts, a sigh drawn from deep within. Then, he prayed for wisdom and the words that he needed. He looked around at the men and ladies gathered there. They have all been hurt with this one, Lord, just like all the other times. I pray each one is the last, but in Your wisdom and plan, it has not been. I always feel like there is something leftover, something not explained. That has been expressed to me as well.

His eyes found Ker, who searched his face and then nodded, a smile on her face. She knows somehow, doesn't she, Lord? Just how she does, I don't know, but You do. Protect this lady and her fellow.

"Now that you have all given your statements, have had a chance to relax, I need to speak. It's not easy what I have to say. Ker, my apologies in advance. I would not want to hurt you, but I think I will."

"It's okay, Dallas. I understand. I think that I have an idea of where you are heading. Just from what I discovered this morning. Go on, please. We need to hear your words."

"Thank you, Ker, for being so gracious. Brody, when you were asked to meet with Keane, you didn't know that he was actually meaning for you to meet with Ker. We have discussed this before. He had hoped and prayed that you would take her to safety. It was not in his plans for you two to be abducted and then dumped out where you were. That was the working of the couple who were behind it all. Ker was taken as a threat against Kelly. You were incidental to it all. The bomb threat that today came from them.

"Ker, your house burnt that day as well. We have determined that your mother had your appliances replaced with gas ones, which you refused. You were to be home that day, but not be aware of what was happening. She had planned to drug you, tamper with the stove, and then let the gas heater pilot light ignite the gas. Thank the Lord that you were not there.

"Your brother was sent away by your father, for the reasons we discussed. It was for his own safety. However, we have determined that he knew more than what he has said. He had been investigating on his own, and your mother found out. She talked out of turn, and again the couple stepped in, kidnapped him, and kept him away from you. Abe and his team found him and brought him home. His collapse today is related to the drugs that he was on. I am sorry to tell you that they damaged his heart. With care, he will make it." He watched as Ker turned into Brody, her shoulders shaking with her sobs.

"I'm so sorry, Ker. Now, just to continue. We have investigated your father's agency. It was what you said. He had turned to finding missing children and teens when you were young and that young boy disappeared. He was successful in finding many of them and returning them to their families, with the authorities' help. This caused friction between your parents. It was kept low key until the last few months.

Then for some reason, and we have not been able to determine why your mother changed and began to try and sabotage his work. Part of it was done through the law firm that he pulled out of.

"Your parents' papers will be returned to you. There was nothing in them that indicated anything but what they were. We are sorry that your father disappeared and we were not able to find him in time. That is a regret we will live with.

"Your mother's killer has been apprehended. He worked for Lowe. Someone saw something and finally came forward. Again, Ker, we are sorry for that loss.

"Now, on to the couple that was behind this. I will give some background and then go on with what we have found. This couple lost a child to an abduction and resulting death when she was only five. She was searched for, your father being part of the search. They blamed him for not finding her when he could find others. However, at that time, technology was not what it is today. The availability of the resources that we have today precluded finding her. It didn't matter to them. They approached your mother with something that she had done illegally as a teen and began to blackmail her. But then, she began to see the advantage of working with them and the lure of financial gain caught her up in it all.

"She made no effort to escape it. In fact, we have documentation that she planned a number of the abductions, using your father as a sounding board. She left this documentation in a safe that you likely didn't know about. Keefe was able to tell us about that a day or so ago. We obtained the warrants and went in and retrieved it.

"Now, Lowe. He is an interesting man. He was never part of the abductions but worked strictly in what you would term as enforcement for the couple. He ensured that the people that they employed did exactly what they were to. He has been tracking you, Ker, over the last few months, finally approaching you and Brody. He has admitted that he planted the bomb on your truck, Brody, more as a scare tactic. He thought it would drive you from investigating."

"He didn't know us very well, now did he?" Brody's face held the sorrow that he was feeling. "He talked the talk well, but there was always something that didn't sit right. I talked to Cadee's father and he never made it to the shelter, even though someone pretended to be him and did."

"That's what we have determined. There are still avenues that we need to investigate, charges to determine, children and teens to find, if we can." Dallas stopped his speech, choking up for a moment, knowing that he had to name the couple.

"The couple, Dallas? Who were they?" Ker's voice was soft but sounded loud in the silence of the room.

"The couple?" Dallas exchanged a look with Barnabas and then Bruce, who had entered with the fellows. "It is a couple that you all know well. They are part of our church. Stan and Lou Clare."

"Stan and Lou?" Buckley's voice could be heard through the muttering before he nodded. "Yes, I can see that. They tried but tried too hard."

A month later, Ker sat contentedly on the balcony outside Brody's office, wrapped up in her favourite afghan, one he had bought her. It had a verse on it that she loved, simply stating that God would be found when He was searched for with all one's heart. I did that, didn't I, Lord? I searched for You for years. It took this adventure, as we call it, with Brody for me to find you in a new and richer way. She turned her head as she heard the door open and then felt herself scooped up into beloved arms and cuddled down on Brody's knee, a favourite activity of theirs.

"All done?" Her head went down on his shoulder and she felt his kiss on the top of it.

"I am. I talked to my employer. We can leave on Monday for our time in the cabin that he offered us."

"That was so nice of him."

"It's rough, he says. Running water and electricity, but they didn't do fancy when they built it."

"That's okay. If you're with me, that's all I need."

Their voices died away for a while, as they watched the sunset spread out over the lake. They had spent many a night wandering the shoreline, watching the freighters as they moved through it, studying the opposite shoreline.

"Ker? Have you decided what you want to do?" Brody wasn't pushing her but he was curious.

"We've talked about that so many times. I'm still not sure, sweetheart. Cadee's parents have asked me to help them at the shelter. And then there's the youth shelter as well. I might give a day or so to each." Ker raised her head to watch his face. "What do you think?"

"I think that you pray about it, take the time that you need to make your decision, we discuss it, and then you decide. There's no rush. I kind of like having you around here when I'm working at home."

"You do, do you? I like that too. When I think of my parents, Mom really didn't want Dad around. Keefe has mentioned it as well."

"Probably because of what she was involved with. I talked to Keefe a while ago. He asked about the memorial service if you still wanted one."

Ker shrugged. "I am not sure. There would only be the ones from here, and they didn't know Dad and Mom. Keefe and I have talked. Given what Mom did, we don't think it's appropriate. We want to for Dad but it's hard."

"We know. How be we just do something simple here in the chapel? With our friends. Buckley would speak, he has already told me that."

"He talked to me. He has a wild sense of humour, did you know that?"

Brody began to laugh. "He always has. Part of his western heritage, I suspect." Brody reached to kiss her, his hand lingering on her face. "I love you, Mrs. Corcoran."

"And I love you, too, Mr. Corcoran. I never dreamt that day you walked into the office that we would have such an adventure, and end up married to the one that God had planned all those years for us."

"Nor did I. I am thankful that I was there. And I am thankful that you are here, Kitten." He reached into a pocket and pulled out a little calico kitten. "With your nickname, I thought maybe you would like a real kitten."

Ker's face lit up and then softened as she reached to kiss him and then took the kitten, holding her against her face, hearing the contented purr from the little bundle of fur. "Thank you, sweetheart. This is what we needed for our family."

Dear Readers:

Thank you for picking up the story of Brody and his Ker. Once more the characters had led the story, throwing in twists and turns along the way. Ker's mother was not meant to be one of the "bad guys" but that is how it happens at times. It is always interesting to see who they decide is the culprit.

Seeking for God is a daily task that we need to do. We seek Him first for salvation. Then, we seek Him to grow in our faith, to understand His word, to know what He wants us to do. Seeking takes many different aspects, depending on the person, and just where they are in their life's walk.

Abe and Emma and his full team just had to show up again. I love it when the characters walk back and forth between books. Their stories are in the *His Guardians* series. The psychologist mentioned is Darcie. Her story and that of her husband Doug's is *The Heart of a Lion*.

God bless each one of you as you seek Him and search for Him with all your heart, finding a treasure that cannot be replaced.

Ronna